"So—you are Philippa."

"Yes." She swallowed, staring at him as if mesmerized, aware that her throat was dry, and that her pulses were doing disturbing things. "And you are—Monsieur de Courcy."

He smiled briefly and sardonically. "Oh, I think, in the circumstances, we should be less formal, perhaps. My name is Alain."

"What circumstances?" Suddenly she was afraid. "I—I don't understand, *monsieur*."

"You have not been told?" The green eyes met hers, held them. "Then the task—the privilege is mine, it seems. You and I, *mademoiselle*, are destined to be married."

SARA CRAVEN probably had the ideal upbringing for a budding writer. She grew up by the seaside in a house crammed with books, a box of old clothes to dress up in and a swing outside in a walled garden. She produced the opening of her first book at age five and is eternally grateful to her mother for having kept a straight face. Now she has more than twenty-five novels to her credit. The author is married and has two children.

Books by Sara Craven

HARLEQUIN PRESENTS
1143—DEVIL AND THE DEEP SEA
1176—KING OF SWORDS
1241—ISLAND OF THE HEART
1279—FLAWLESS
1330—STORM FORCE
1471—WHEN THE DEVIL DRIVES

SARA CRAVEN

Desperate Measures

Harlequin Books

TORONTO • NEW YORK • LONDON
AMSTERDAM • PARIS • SYDNEY • HAMBURG
STOCKHOLM • ATHENS • TOKYO • MILAN
MADRID • WARSAW • BUDAPEST • AUCKLAND

Harlequin Presents first edition November 1992
ISBN 0-373-11503-2

Original hardcover edition published in 1991
by Mills & Boon Limited

DESPERATE MEASURES

CHAPTER ONE

'But this treatment is totally revolutionary! The specialist says it could make all the difference to Daddy—that it might even cure him permanently. But it's expensive, and it's in America, and we just don't have that kind of money.'

Philippa Roscoe leaned forward, her hazel eyes fixed pleadingly on her former stepmother's unresponsive face. 'Monica, you're the only one I can turn to. Help us—please!'

'It's quite impossible.' Lady Underhay shook her head with finality. 'I haven't access to unlimited funds, Philippa, and I certainly can't ask Lennox for money to go to my ex-husband.' She flushed, looking self-conscious. 'He's always been—a little jealous of Gavin.'

'They were business partners once.'

'But that was some time ago. And anyway, Lennox feels the board was more than generous when Gavin left—deserted them in that absurd way to go off and paint.' Monica's lips became set. 'Deserted me, as well.'

You were the one who left! Philippa wanted to cry out. You were the one who wouldn't risk your lifestyle to let Daddy fulfil his dream. And now here you are, once more, living in the lap of luxury.

But she said none of it. Across the years, she could remember her father's face, haggard with the strain, his voice telling her huskily, 'You mustn't blame

5

Monica, sweetheart, and you mustn't be bitter either. I'm trying not to be. She loved us, in her way, but she can't do without money and comfort. She needs it as other people need air to breathe. And, inevitably, she'll go where money is. Lennox will treat her well. They have a mutual regard for material possessions and security.'

Looking round the elegant drawing-room, Philippa could well believe it. The sale of any of the pictures and antiques it contained would have paid for Gavin Roscoe's treatment.

'Anyway, I understood that your father had been quite successful at this precious painting of his. Can't he produce a few more pictures—pot-boilers or something, to finance his own treatment?' Monica looked restively at her watch.

Philippa shook her head, thankful that Gavin couldn't hear her. 'The disease—or rather the virus that caused it—attacked the muscles on his right side first. He has—difficulty using his hand, so he can't paint any more.'

Monica bit deeply into the coral curve of her lower lip. 'I—see. Well, that is tragic, but of course, if he'd remained with the firm, there'd have been private health insurance to cover this kind of eventuality.' She shook her head. 'I'm sorry, my dear, I really am, but there's nothing I can do.'

Philippa's hands twisted together in her lap, the knuckles white. 'Monica, I've got to get that money somehow. I've got to make sure Daddy has this chance before it's too late. The specialist says if there's any more muscle wastage...' She paused, her voice breaking. 'I'll do anything—agree to any terms you offer. I'll pay the loan back, if it takes the rest of my life, but I've got to have it. If you ever cared for Daddy at all, please help me to think of some way.'

Monica flushed again. 'Naturally I cared. But what you ask is out of the question.' She paused. 'Have you approached some financial institution?'

'I tried, but I had nothing to use as collateral for a loan. I can't even guarantee there'll be a lasting cure, or that Daddy will ever be able to paint again.'

'What a pity Gavin didn't make some provision for the future before throwing up his business career in that crazy way.' Monica's tone was short.

'He couldn't know he was going to be ill,' Philippa protested. 'He was so well up to that winter—happier than he'd ever been...' She stopped guiltily, aware that her words were singularly infelicitous, and saw by the tightening of Lady Underhay's facial muscles that she thought so too.

'I'm afraid I'm going to have to ask you to leave,' she said, getting to her feet. 'Lennox will be home at any minute, and I'd as soon he didn't find you here. We're entertaining this evening—the head of De Courcy International, as it happens—and there are things I must do.' She paused. 'I'm sincerely sorry I can't help, Philippa, but there's really nothing I can suggest.' She hesitated again. 'Surely there must be similar treatment available in this country on the National Health Service, for instance?'

'No, as I've told you this is completely new. In fact, it's still at the experimental stage,' Philippa said tonelessly, rising in her turn. 'I'm sorry to have troubled you. You were my last hope.'

As she turned to the door, it opened and Lennox Underhay came in. He checked at the sight of her.

'Philippa, isn't it? How are you?' His smile was polite but unenthusiastic, and the look he threw his wife was questioning.

'She has to rush away, darling,' Monica intercepted hastily. She put her arm through Philippa's. 'I'll see you out, my dear.'

Her lips were compressed when they reached the hall. 'No doubt he'll want to know what you were doing here,' she said snappishly. 'I don't want to seem uncaring, Philippa, and I feel for you in your distress, but you do make things very awkward sometimes.'

'I wouldn't have come here if I hadn't been absolutely desperate,' Philippa said quietly. She handed Lady Underhay a scrap of paper. 'This is the telephone number of my hotel. If you do happen to think of something—some way in which I could raise the money, you can reach me there over the next couple of days.'

Monica accepted it with a reluctant sigh. 'Very well, but I'm promising nothing.'

Life was so unfair, Philippa thought bitterly as she rode home on the Tube. Monica had simply exchanged one luxuriously cushioned setting for another. If leaving Gavin after five years of marriage had caused her any real grief, she'd kept it well concealed. But it had probably been outweighed by her sense of injury at his decision. When Monica was getting her own way, no one could be sweeter. But when she was crossed . . .

Philippa grimaced inwardly. Gavin, a widower for some years, had indulged and cosseted his second wife, and she'd revelled in it. When Gavin had first announced his intention of giving up his City directorships, his home in London and country house in West Sussex in order to be an artist, Monica had treated it as a bad joke, then as a temporary aberration. When she'd realised he was not only serious, but absolutely determined, she had become angry, and Philippa still shuddered when she recalled the scenes and tantrums, all of which Gavin had borne patiently.

Anyway, Monica had fallen on her feet, firstly with an over-generous divorce settlement, which she seemed conveniently to have forgotten, and later with Lennox Underhay, who had always admired her chic blonde prettiness.

But, at first, everything had worked out for Gavin too. Instead of starving in some foreign gutter as Monica had confidently predicted, he had found a ready and high-paying market for his landscapes, and he and Philippa had enjoyed several heady years of travelling round the Dordogne and Provence together as he worked. Gavin Roscoe, as one critic had said, had a unique ability to express in paint the intensity of heat and shade the southern regions of France could produce.

It had seemed as though it would never end, Philippa thought, biting her lower lip until she could taste blood. Perhaps it was as well that neither of them had realised how little time there really was.

I'm not going to think like that, she castigated herself. I'm going to get the money, somehow, and Daddy's going to America for this treatment.

But how could she get rich quick? she wondered, leaning her aching forehead against the train window. There were so few avenues left unexplored.

I've tried all the conventional ways, she thought. Maybe I should consider more desperate measures.

High-class call-girls earn a lot, it's said, and it's tax-free. She turned her head a little, studying her reflection in the glass. Only a supreme optimist would think the punters were clamouring for skinny nineteen-year-olds with small breasts, straight hair and very little experience.

Let's face it, she thought. No experience at all.

She was thankful her father had no idea what she was contemplating, even in joke. He thought she was trying to sell the last painting he'd produced before the muscle wastage became too severe.

But even that had been hopeless. The man at the Orbis Gallery had been very kind, very understanding, but the painting had been almost unrecognisable as Gavin Roscoe's work. It had been unrealistic to think they might take it.

I'm going to need a miracle, Philippa thought.

She was stretched on the bed in her tiny single room a few hours later, trying to interest herself in a detective story she'd bought at the station, when the phone rang.

It was probably reception checking when she was leaving, she thought as she lifted the receiver.

Instead, her stepmother's voice said curtly, 'Can you come over to the house right away? There's something I want to discuss with you.'

'Something about the money.' Philippa's heart skipped a beat. 'You mean you've thought of a way?'

'Possibly.'

'But that's wonderful! What is it?'

'It's not something I care to talk about on the telephone,' Monica returned frostily. 'As for it being wonderful—well, that remains to be seen.' She paused.

'It would help if you came looking reasonably presentable.' She replaced the receiver.

Presentable, Philippa thought with bewilderment, reviewing in her mind the details of the scanty wardrobe she'd brought with her. There was little there that would fall within Monica's stringent requirements.

She compromised with clean jeans, and a cream full-sleeved shirt, brushing her brown hair until it shone, then fastening it behind her ears with two tortoiseshell combs.

She took a cab to Lowden Square. She found Monica alone, standing by the marble fireplace in the drawing-room, brandy glass in hand. She turned as Philippa was shown in, and her lips thinned. 'My God, I said presentable, and you turn up looking like some art student!'

'Which is exactly what I am,' Philippa returned, lifting her chin. 'Anyway, do my clothes really matter so much? I'm not going to be offered a modelling contract, surely?'

'There's no guarantee you're going to be offered anything at all,' Monica said with a snap. 'When he sees you, he may well have second thoughts, and who can blame him?'

'He?' Philippa frowned. 'Just who is he?'

'He is Alain de Courcy,' Monica said shortly. 'As I think I mentioned, he's the head of De Courcy International, and he has a proposition to put to you. If you're as desperate for money as you claim to be, you'll listen to him, although I find the whole thing totally incredible—unthinkable.' She drank some of her brandy. 'He's waiting for you in the library, so I suggest you don't keep him waiting any longer.'

Philippa walked the few yards to the library, her mind whirling. She had rarely seen her stepmother so on edge—not since the time she'd first learned Gavin's plans for the future. Obviously the important dinner party hadn't gone precisely to plan.

She'd heard of de Courcy International, of course. Who hadn't? But what on earth could anyone connected with such a vast and influential organisation want with someone as insignificant as herself? As Monica had indicated, it made no sense.

She paused outside the library door, wondering whether she should knock, then, deciding against it, turned the handle and walked into the room.

All the lights were on, and Philippa paused, blinking a little after the relative dimness of the hall. Then, as her eyes grew accustomed to the glare, and she saw him, she stopped dead, completely taken aback.

The head of an important company like De Courcy should be an older man, she found herself thinking dazedly. Someone heavyweight, middle-aged and mature—like Lennox Underhay, for instance.

But this man was young, and she realised, incredibly attractive, as her artist's eye took in the underlying strength of his superb bone-structure which would last long after his surface looks were gone. The thick dark hair, waving back from his forehead, the green eyes with their almost feminine sweep of lashes, the firm-lipped mouth and deeply cleft chin—all these were only a bonus.

He was tall too, his broad-shouldered, lean-hipped body perfectly set off by the formal elegance of his evening clothes.

He looked surprised as well, the dark brows snapping together autocratically above his high-bridged nose as he looked her unhurriedly up and down.

Philippa's hands felt damp suddenly, and she wiped her palms on her jeans. The movement broke the silent stillness which seemed to enclose them, and he moved too, suddenly, abruptly, as if he was angry about something.

But when he spoke, his cool, faintly accented voice was only meditative. 'So—you are Philippa.'

'Yes.' She swallowed, still staring at him as if mesmerised, aware that her throat was dry, and that her pulses were doing disturbing things. 'And you are—Monsieur de Courcy.'

He smiled briefly and sardonically. 'Oh, I think, in the circumstances, we should be less formal, perhaps. My name is Alain.'

'What circumstances?' Suddenly she was afraid. I didn't mean what I said about being a high-class call-girl, she placated some unknown but clearly humourless deity. 'I—I don't understand, *monsieur*.'

'You have not been told?' The green eyes met hers, held them. 'Then the task—the privilege is mine, it seems. You and I, *mademoiselle*, are destined to be married.'

For a moment, Philippa's mind seemed numb. She couldn't move or speak—or even think coherently. Incredible, Monica had said. But it was worse than that. It was completely insane. The word kept running through her brain. The head of De Courcy International had gone stark raving mad, and they were the only ones who knew.

'You had better sit,' Alain de Courcy added curtly. 'Before you fall down.' His gaze raked her again, taking in the cling of the tight-fitting jeans to her slender hips, the slight swell of her breasts under the thin shirt. The frown returned. 'How old are you, *mademoiselle*?'

'I'm—nearly twenty.' She ran her tongue round her dry lips. 'Did you really say—married?'

He nodded unsmilingly.

She swallowed. 'But I've never seen you before in my life—never even knew you existed until tonight.'

'Nor I you,' he said with a slight shrug. 'But that need not be an obstacle.' He fetched a high-backed chair and set it for her, then placed another one opposite for himself. 'Before you reject me out of hand as a dangerous lunatic, allow me to explain. I need to be married, *mademoiselle*, and urgently too. Before I came to dinner tonight, I was seriously contemplating advertising for a wife in some newspaper.'

'This must be some tasteless joke,' Philippa said thickly. 'I shall never forgive Monica—or Lennox. I suppose it was because I made a nuisance of myself earlier—said I was desperate for money.'

'There is no joke,' Alain de Courcy said quietly. 'I was *distrait* at dinner, and they persuaded me to speak of my problems. It was then that your stepmother suggested that your dilemma might provide the solution to mine. This is why you were asked to come here tonight. This is why we are alone together now.'

She took a breath. 'I—can't believe this. It's crazy!' She sent him a scornful look. 'Putting an ad in a paper, indeed! You're the last person in the world who needs to resort to something like that.'

He smiled faintly. '*Merci du compliment*—if that's what it was. But the truth is, I know very few women of a suitable age and background and even fewer who would allow themselves to be taken in marriage in such a headlong way, without a conventional period of courtship at least—if not vows of undying love and devotion. Anything less, however insincere, would insult them.'

'You don't think it would insult me?' Philippa stiffened.

Alain de Courcy shrugged. 'From what little I have learned tonight, I don't think you can afford to be insulted,' he countered levelly. 'I understand you need a substantial sum of money to pay for your father's medical treatment in the United States, and maintain him there in a private clinic. If you marry me, I will make sure sufficient funds are made available for you to use in this way—or as you wish.' He paused. 'You need me for your father's future, *mademoiselle*. I need you for mine. Do we have a bargain?'

Monica had said, 'Listen to him.' Philippa found herself shivering.

'First, you'd better explain why you need to be married so quickly,' she said. 'Why can't you wait—find a wife whom you might—care for?'

'Marriage, *ma chère*, is a lottery,' he said cynically. 'Until now I have always managed to avoid buying a ticket. But now I find myself under pressure through my family.'

He paused. 'I inherited the chair of De Courcy International from my grandfather. Since then, my uncle Louis has always borne a grudge that he was passed over for me. For the past two years, he has been working against me, trying to thwart deals I was involved in—attempting to undermine my authority by castigating me to the more sober members of my board as an irresponsible playboy.'

He shot her a swift glance. 'You smile at last, *mademoiselle*, and I too found the situation amusing—once. But lately it has become altogether more serious. My name has recently been linked with a woman, who is married to a man of importance in the government. There have been hints in the papers— rumours and innuendo in the circles I move in.'

He shrugged. 'There has been gossip before—I am not a saint—but this time my uncle has managed to gain support for his opinion that my conduct is a disgrace, and that, through me, De Courcy International is likely to be plunged into a major scandal with all kinds of repercussions. I am, he says, unfit to be chairman any longer.

'Accordingly, he has called an emergency meeting in two weeks' time to discuss the situation, and call for my resignation. He plans to become chairman in my place, against my grandfather's expressed wish, and that is now a distinct possibility. You must believe that it would also be a disaster. You see my problem?'

Philippa bit her lip. 'I—suppose so. But maybe your uncle's right—perhaps you are irresponsible. After all, if you're having an affair with this woman—neglecting the company for her...'

His mouth twisted. 'My uncle, *mademoiselle*, has an insufferably bourgeois mind. My private life has no bearing on my role as head of De Courcy. No woman has ever come between me and my work, or ever will.'

He hesitated, his expression rueful. 'There is an additional factor. My uncle has a daughter, Sidonie. He has dropped unmistakable hints that if I were to offer marriage to my cousin his opposition to me would cease immediately.'

'Then isn't that the obvious solution?'

'You would not suggest such a thing if you had ever met my cousin Sidonie. She has a bad complexion, and the disposition of a jealous shrew.'

Philippa bit her lip. 'I might be just as bad.'

'That is a risk I shall have to take.' His eyes swept with disturbing candour over her face, and down her body. 'Your skin at least is clear—what I can see of it. And you are also a loyal and loving daughter, or so Lady Underhay assures me. That is why she and her husband suggested I should have this interview with you.'

He paused. 'We both have dire problems, *mademoiselle*, and to solve them, only desperate measures will do. Agreed?'

Desperate measures, she thought. Her own words come back to haunt her.

'Well—perhaps.' She spread her hands helplessly. 'But—marriage . . .'

He studied her for a long moment. 'The implications of that word deter you, *peut-être*. You wish to be reassured about the exact nature of the relationship I am offering?'

Philippa found she was blushing to the roots of her hair. 'Yes.'

'Well, that is natural.' He was silent for a moment. 'I am not a savage, Philippa, but at the same time I need to ensure that the de Courcy name continues to the next generation. I will, one day, ask you to give me a son. But you will be given time—as much as you need—to—accustom yourself before that happens. Is that the assurance you require?'

'Yes—no—I don't know.' Philippa gripped her hands together. 'Oh, this is ridiculous—an impossible situation!'

'As you say. But it is also a practical solution to our mutual difficulties.'

'And that's all that matters?'

'What else is there?' He sounded amused.

'What about—love?'

'What about it, indeed?' He was laughing openly now. His teeth were very white, she noticed irrelevantly. 'But as you mentioned earlier, *mademoiselle*, we have only just met. I feel any declaration of passion on my part would be premature...'

'I didn't mean that,' she said angrily.

'No? Then are you telling me there is already an important relationship in your life?'

The frankly sceptical note in his voice grated on her, and she lifted her chin, her blush deepening hectically.

'Is it so impossible?'

'It is unlikely,' he said with infuriating calmness. 'You have a disturbingly—untouched quality.'

She glared at him. 'As a matter of fact, I was really wondering what would happen if, after we were married, one of us—both of us—met someone else.'

'Marriage is not always a barrier to such relationships,' he said softly. 'As long as discretion is maintained.'

'That's an abominably cynical point of view!'

'And, again, I thought I was being practical,' Alain de Courcy retorted. 'In any event, we are not yet married, so why look for difficulties where there are none?'

'Oh, of course, everything's going to be plain sailing,' Philippa flung back at him scathingly. 'I can see that.'

He was silent for a long moment, then he said levelly, 'Philippa, marriage is never easy. Even if we had met and fallen madly in love, there would still have to be—adjustments. Our situation is unusual, perhaps, but who can say that a marriage which springs from mutual convenience and friendship cannot succeed eventually?'

'Except that we're not friends,' she said in a stifled voice.

'Not yet, perhaps, but is the prospect so impossible?'

'Almost completely, I'd have said.' She shook her head. 'Oh, there must be someone else you can ask.'

He shrugged. 'As I have said, I can always advertise. But to whom will you go for the money that you need with such desperation? Or did your stepmother exaggerate this?'

'No.' Philippa bent her head wretchedly. 'She was quite right. Only—I just didn't think it would—come to this.' She glanced at him. 'You—wouldn't consider just—lending me the money.'

'Only with a marriage certificate for security. I want to buy instant respectability from you, *ma chérie*. I spend a lot of my time in your country. I propose to tell my family and friends that we met on a previous visit, and I have been courting you ever since. We kept our marriage private because of your father's ill health.' He snapped his fingers. '*Voilà!* All the rumours silenced at one blow.'

She sighed deeply. 'It isn't that simple. I can't answer you now—tonight. You've got to let me have time to think—to decide . . .'

'That is reasonable. I am staying at the Savoy Hotel. You may contact me there.' He got to his feet, and she followed suit. 'But don't keep me waiting too long, *mademoiselle*. For both of us, time is of the essence.' He paused. 'Would it make any difference if I told you I possess one of your father's pictures?'

'Oh?' Her lips parted in renewed astonishment. 'Which one?'

'*The Bridge at Montascaux*. It would be a pity to let such talent and vigour—waste away.' He allowed his words to sink in for a few seconds, then smiled at her. 'Now, may I drive you home?'

'Oh, no, thank you.' Philippa took an involuntary step backwards away from him. She felt as if she'd been inadvertently locked into a cage with a tiger, and lucky to escape with her life.

But if I marry him, she thought, panic closing her throat, there'll be no escape. I shall have to live with him—share a roof. Eventually—a bed.

Her mind blanked off, refusing to accept such a possibility.

Yet there was the money for Gavin—available for her, as he'd promised. That was what she had to remember. She needed a miracle, and perhaps that was what she was being offered.

But it didn't feel like any miracle. It felt like a two-edged sword—dangerous and unpredictable. I am no saint, he had said, and she could well believe it.

She realised he was watching her closely, the green eyes narrowed, and hurried into speech.

'I'll let you know tomorrow what I decide—I promise.'

'Then I shall wait impatiently until then.' He strolled across to her, and before she realised what he intended, lifted her hand briefly to his lips. The contact was fleeting, but she felt as if her flesh had been seared.

He looked down at her, smiling faintly into her eyes. He said softly, 'I wish you a restful night, *ma chère*. And if you cannot sleep, think well.'

CHAPTER TWO

WHEN she awoke the following morning to pale sunlight filtering through the curtains, Philippa thought at first it had all been some wild, preposterous dream.

Things like that just didn't happen, she told herself, huddling under the covers. Not in real life. A girl like herself, with no particular looks to recommend her, couldn't possibly receive an offer of marriage from a French millionaire for any reason whatever, no matter how practical it had been made to sound. She tried to recall to mind exactly what he'd said, but her brain refused to co-operate, producing only a jumble of confused impressions.

It must have been a dream, she told herself foggily. My worries and the name of Monica's dinner guest just got muddled in my subconscious, that's all. There's a logical explanation for everything.

She stretched her arms above her head, then brought them down slowly in front of her. She had small, workmanlike hands, which she was accustomed to seeing stained with paint. Latterly, though, she'd been using them mainly to help nurse Gavin, and they looked almost respectable for once.

Suddenly, as she looked at them, one of the images in her mind sharpened into a reality she couldn't ignore. She sat bolt upright, stifling a startled yelp.

My God, she thought, he kissed my hand! She sat for a moment, staring at her fingers, as if she expected to see them marked with the brand of Cain—re-living

22

with shock the swift brush of his mouth against her skin. Knowing helplessly there was no way in which she could have dreamed that particular sensation.

It happened, she thought. It all really happened. And, in that case, what the hell do I do now?

Well, first she could answer the phone, which rang at that moment as if obeying some cue.

'Well?' was Monica's response to her guarded 'Hello.'

Philippa swallowed. 'Well what?' she countered feebly.

Monica sighed irritably. 'Please don't behave as if you're half-witted,' she commanded crisply. 'What have you decided? Are you going to accept Alain de Courcy's offer?'

There were dust motes whirling in the broad beam of sunlight slanting between the thin curtains.

That's what I feel like, Philippa thought, gripping the receiver as if it was her sole contact with reality. As if I've been caught up in something I don't understand and can't control, and now I'm helpless—going round and round forever.

'Philippa?' Monica's impatient voice sounded in her ear. 'Hello—are you still there? I asked what you were going to do.'

She said quietly, 'I don't think I really have a choice. I'm going to—to take his money.'

'Not merely the money, my dear.' Monica gave a short laugh. 'You'll also be getting an exquisite Paris apartment, a country house near Fountainebleau, and a villa in the hills above Nice, and that's just to start with. And Alain is one of the most attractive and eligible bachelors in France. You're doing extremely well for yourself.'

'Am I?' Philippa asked. Her heart felt like a stone.

'You'd better be married from Lowden Square,' Monica went on. 'Will Gavin be well enough to attend the ceremony?'

Philippa sat up as if she'd been shot. 'No,' she said. 'No, I'm afraid not. I hope by the time it takes place he'll already be in America, starting his treatment.'

'Well, just as you wish, of course. I'll have a room prepared for you, and expect you some time later today. We're going to have to do some serious shopping.'

'Why?'

Monica's sigh quivered with irritation. 'My dear girl, although the ceremony will undoubtedly be very quiet, and extremely private, you still cannot be married in denim jeans. Lennox and I will supply your trousseau as our gift.'

'It really isn't necessary...'

'Nonsense,' Monica said crisply. 'I'll see you later.' And rang off.

An hour later, Philippa found herself being shown into Alain de Courcy's hotel suite. He was sitting at a table by the window, eating breakfast and reading a newspaper, as she entered, but he rose to his feet immediately, greeting her courteously.

'I'm sorry,' Philippa said when they were alone. 'I should have telephoned first. I'm obviously too early...'

Pas du tout. He motioned her to the seat on the other side of the table. 'Have you eaten?'

Philippa realised with embarrassment that the table was laid for two. 'Oh—you're expecting company as well.'

He smiled at her. He was casually dressed this morning, she noticed, in slim-fitting dark blue pants and a matching shirt, open at the neck to reveal the tanned column of his throat, and the first shadowing of hair on his chest.

He said, 'I was expecting you, *ma chère*. Will you have some coffee?' He lifted the pot and poured some into the other cup, then offered her cream and sugar which she refused.

Alain de Courcy took an apple from the bowl of fruit which had accompanied his breakfast and began to peel it.

'You've had sufficient time to think?'

She nodded wordlessly.

'So—what is your answer?'

She picked up the spoon and aimlessly stirred the dark aromatic brew in her cup, deliberately not looking at him.

'I—will marry you, *monsieur*.' She paused. 'But there are conditions.'

'I imagined there might be,' he said with a certain irony. 'Tell me about them.'

She said, 'My father's treatment is to start as soon as possible—and he's to know nothing about our— arrangement.'

'You are going to keep our marriage a secret from him? But why?'

'Because he'd know why I was doing it, and he'd refuse to go to America—to let me sacrifice myself for him. I can't risk that happening.'

'I understand, but I am not sure you will be able to carry it through. There will come a time when he has to know.'

Philippa flushed dully. 'You mean when—if I get pregnant? I'll cross that bridge when I come to it.'

'I did not entirely mean that,' Alain said slowly. 'If the treatment is successful, he will wish to take up his former life again, and you were a close part of that. Don't you think he might notice you had acquired a husband?'

She said quietly, 'If the treatment works—when he's fully recovered, I'll tell him everything, because it will be too late then for him to object, and I hope he'll understand why I had to do it.' She paused, biting her lip. 'If it doesn't work, then it won't matter anyway.'

She hesitated again. 'Also, I was wondering whether you wanted me to have a medical examination.'

He put down the quarter of apple he was eating and stared at her. 'Why should I wish such a thing? Are you feeling unwell? Do you believe your father's illness is hereditary in some way?'

'Oh, no.' Philippa's face was like a peony. 'I was thinking over what you said about wanting a—a child—an heir. I thought maybe you'd want to check that I was capable . . .'

Alain lifted a hand and stemmed the halting words. 'You are not some brood animal that I am purchasing,' he said bitingly. 'I think, when the time comes, that nature should be allowed to take its course, don't you?'

She mumbled something in acute embarrassment.

'I can't hear you,' he said with faint impatience. 'And why don't you look at me when you speak?'

She gave him a despairing glance. 'I said—this is never going to work. I mean, no one in their right mind is ever—ever going to believe in this marriage.'

'*Pourquoi pas?*'

'Well, just look at me!'

'I am looking,' he said. 'You are a little underweight, and your hair needs cutting. What else is there to say?'

Philippa's hands clasped together tensely in her lap. 'I don't feel like anyone's wife—especially someone who's a millionaire and has got houses dotted all over France. I don't know what you expect...'

'Believe me, I expect very little. At the beginning it will be enough that you exist—that you appear in public at my side.' He shrugged. 'As for my homes—I employ efficient staff.' He gave her an ironic glance. 'You will not have to keep the rooms clean or cook for me.'

'But you'll want me to act as hostess when you entertain—and I've never done anything like that before.' Her voice broke a little as she remembered the endless sun-drenched days with Gavin in the southwest of France, the casual camaraderie, the street markets and the tiny bistros.

'You can speak,' he said. 'You can express yourself articulately. But I would be at your side—and I would naturally warn you if there were any topics of conversation best avoided with particular people.'

'And I'd have to wear—different clothes.'

His mouth twisted in faint amusement. 'Did you plan to spend the rest of your life in those deplorable jeans, *ma petite*?'

'Of course not.' Philippa was silent for a moment, then said jerkily, 'I don't think you realise just how fundamentally my whole life is going to change.'

'Mine also. Marriage as a concept has no more appeal for me than for you, *ma chère*.'

'Well, I still think it would make more sense if you married your cousin Sidonie,' she said stubbornly, drinking the last of her coffee. 'She must know you don't care for her, and if she's prepared to pretend...'

'But she is not,' Alain said coldly. 'She would wish me to do so, however. She would expect me to act as if I was madly in love with her—to explain every absence from her side each minute of the day and night in order to spare myself tears, temper and jealous scenes. I would find that wearing in the extreme.'

'I can imagine,' Philippa said sarcastically. 'I gather I'm not supposed to ask questions?'

'Ask whatever you want, *ma chère*.' He gave her an enigmatic look. 'But don't blame me if you do not like the answers.'

He pushed back his chair and rose. 'And now we have a busy day ahead of us. I will contact my lawyers, and the London branch of my bank, and arrange to have a preliminary payment made to you for your father's expenses.' He walked round the table and stood looking at her with a slight smile. 'You will not, I hope, take the money and run, *chérie*. Because that would not amuse me at all.'

'I'll keep my word.' Philippa lifted her chin. 'We shall just have to—trust each other, *monsieur*.'

'So it seems.' He held out his hand. 'Shall we seal our bargain in the usual way?'

Reluctantly, she allowed his fingers to encompass hers, and, shocked, found herself drawn forward before she could resist. Alain's arm went round her, anchoring her against him, and she felt the firm, cool pressure of his mouth on hers.

She tried desperately to pull away, but he would not allow it. If she'd been tempted to think of him as an effete businessman, she now realised her mistake. His muscles were like iron.

Yet his lips were silk, she realised with a kind of wonder, moving gently and persuasively on hers. Coaxing her. Tempting her...

The kiss could only have lasted a few seconds, but it seemed an eternity before he raised his head.

When she could speak, she said thickly, 'You—shouldn't have done that.'

'No, I shouldn't,' he agreed, running a rueful hand round his chin. 'I have not shaved yet today, and I have marked you a little. You have delicate skin, *ma belle*. I shall have to remember that.'

'All you need to remember,' Philippa said hotly, 'is that you promised you wouldn't—molest me. That you'd give me time.'

Alain's brows lifted. 'What a fuss about such a chaste salute! Now if I had really kissed you...' He slanted a smile at her. 'Come and talk to me while I shave,' he invited softly. 'And then let us see, *hein*?'

'No.' She took a step backwards, aware that her breathing was flurried, and that he knew it too. 'I—I have to go. I've got to talk to my father—to his specialist—tell them the good news—make arrangements.'

To her relief, he made no attempt to detain her. 'So how do I maintain contact with you?'

'I'll be at Lowden Square. Monica has invited me to stay with her—until the wedding.'

He nodded. 'Then I will see you there. *Au revoir*.'

Until we meet again, Philippa thought wretchedly when she was safely outside in the corridor with the door closed between them. She stood for a moment, allowing her hammering heartbeat to abate slightly.

But she wasn't at all sure she wanted to meet someone as disturbing as Alain de Courcy again especially under the circumstances to which she was now committed.

I wish, she thought, that we had just said—goodbye.

A week later, she saw her father leave for America in the care of a private nurse. She'd invented a story that some money had been left inadvertently in a company pension plan. She wasn't sure he believed her, and if he had been well he would probably have asked some searching questions. As it was, he was having one of his bad spells, and he was clearly too relieved at the prospect of some treatment to interrogate her too minutely, and she was thankful for that. Three days after his departure, she became the wife of Alain de Courcy.

The days in between had passed in a kind of blur. Philippa retired somewhere inside herself, and allowed events to take charge with a kind of passivity totally foreign to her nature.

But then nothing that was happening seemed to bear any resemblance to real life. She tried on clothes with total detachment, sat in the hairdresser's while her long hair was cut in a sleek and manageable bob, and subtly highlighted, and listened to Monica's impatient chivvying without actually hearing a word she said.

Reality finally impinged when she found herself on a private jet flight to Paris in the chic amber wool going-away dress which Monica had chosen for her. She stared down at the broad gold band on her wedding finger, and tried to remember without success how she'd felt when Alain had placed it there a few hours before.

Numb, she thought. And that was how she still felt.

But at least she did not have a honeymoon to endure. They would have to dispense with that convention for the time being, Alain had told her, because he had already taken more time off to stay in London than he could spare. So they were going straight to his Paris apartment.

'I hope it won't be too dull for you,' he said.

'Oh, no,' Philippa had stammered, hardly able to conceal her relief. Simply sharing a roof with him would be ordeal enough, she thought. The prospect of being alone with him in the bridal suite of some exotic location with all that implied had been more than she could bear. And judging by the sardonic slant of his mouth he'd known exactly what she was thinking.

She put a hand to her throat and touched the string of matched pearls which had been his wedding gift to her.

'Exquisite!' Monica had exclaimed as she helped Philippa to change.

'Yes—but don't they mean tears?' Philippa had felt faintly troubled as she fastened the clasp.

'Not, my dear, if you have any sense.' Monica's smile held a touch of envy not unmixed with malice. 'Enjoy the loot, Madame de Courcy. Because you may find that's all there is,' she added cynically, then glanced at her watch. 'Now do make haste. Your husband's waiting.'

Your husband. Philippa stole a covert look at this unexpected and alarming phenomenon who sat beside her, apparently engrossed in a sheaf of papers from his briefcase.

She didn't know whether to feel glad or aggrieved at his absorption, and decided on balance that even if it wasn't exactly flattering, it was a relief. At least she didn't have to try to make conversation.

During the past ten days she had seen Alain almost daily, but she knew him no better than she'd done that first evening when she'd walked into the library at Lowden Square, she acknowledged ruefully.

To her relief, he had made no further attempt to kiss her, or move their relationship on to a more intimate level than the friendship he'd promised, although they were still really no more than acquaintances, she admitted to herself.

He had been invariably charming to her, however, setting himself, she realised, to draw her out, discovering her tastes in literature and music as well as art, whether she preferred ballet to opera, if she enjoyed tennis or squash, her preferences in food and wine.

It was as if he was compiling a dossier on her. And perhaps he was—a series of facts to be fed into a computer somewhere at De Courcy International and resurrected at birthday or anniversary times.

And she was only just beginning to realise how very little he had vouchsafed in return, this stranger who was now married to her for better or worse.

For better or worse. Philippa repeated the words in her head, and shivered suddenly.

In no time at all, it seemed, they were landing. The formalities at the airport were mercifully brief, then Philippa found herself being whisked away in a chauffeur-driven limousine. She supposed this was the kind of treatment she would have to get accustomed to.

Almost before she was ready, she found herself walking into an imposing building in one of the city's most fashionable areas, and travelling up in the lift to the penthouse.

The apartment, Alain had told her, was not part of the family estate which he had inherited, but had been acquired by himself a few years previously as a *pied-à-terre* near his business headquarters. He was looked after by a married couple, a Madame Henriette Giscard, and her husband Albert, and they were waiting to welcome their master and his new bride, their faces well-trained masks.

When the introductions were completed, Alain took her to one side. 'Will you be all right if I leave you here?' he asked in a low tone. 'I need to go to the office, and I cannot say when it will be possible to return.'

'Oh, that's all right—that's fine,' Philippa stammered, feeling the colour rise in her face under his quizzical look.

'I don't doubt it.' Mouth twisting, Alain ran his forefinger down the curve of her hot cheek. He turned back to Madame Giscard, waiting at a discreet distance. 'I shall not be here for dinner, Henriette. Make sure Madame has everything she requires.' He lifted Philippa's nerveless hand and pressed a swift kiss into its palm. *'Au revoir, mignonne.'*

If the Giscards considered his departure eccentric behaviour for a new bridegroom, they kept their opinions well hidden. Philippa found herself being conducted over the apartment with a certain amount of ceremony. It seemed evident from the covert glances she'd seen them exchanging that not only was the marriage itself a shock to them, but that the Giscards considered her the last kind of wife they would have expected Alain de Courcy to choose. Her lack of sophistication and experience must be woefully apparent, she thought bitterly, and if she couldn't fool the servants, how could she hope to deceive his family and friends?

She managed to contain her sigh of relief when Madame Giscard expressionlessly showed her to her bedroom, a pretty Empire-style room immediately adjoining the one used by Alain himself. In spite of the neutral attitude he had adopted towards her up to now, she had still secretly feared some confrontation over the sleeping arrangements once they were actually married. It was good to know he could be trusted after all.

She requested a light dinner, and was served promptly and without fuss with a cup of *bouillon*, and a perfectly grilled sole with fresh fruit to follow. Afterwards she telephoned the New York clinic, as she always did, to ask after Gavin. She received the usual response—that it was still too early for any definite prognosis—and after that she was left pretty much to her own devices.

She decided to conduct her own, more leisurely exploration of the apartment without Madame Giscard's chilly presence at her side. She found the place slightly austere and unwelcoming, with its large, high-ceilinged rooms, and vaguely reminiscent of Lowden Square in its elegant formality. There was nothing in the least homelike about it, Philippa decided, hearing the clatter of her heels on the polished floor. The furniture and curtains seemed to warn,

'Look, but don't touch.' She found herself wondering how much time Alain actually spent there.

But there was one blessedly familiar touch—Gavin's painting of the bridge at Montascaux which hung over the elegant marble fireplace in the *salon*. She stood, her hands behind her back, staring up at it. She had loved their time at Montascaux. She sighed soundlessly as she remembered the jumble of roofs on the steep hillside sweeping down to the river, with the ruined château towering above the gorge. They'd rented a house high above the village, with a wood behind it. The house in the clouds, she thought nostalgically. While Gavin painted, Philippa had done her own sketching, then shopped at the small but cheerful market, concocting what she now recognised must have been some weird and wonderful meals for them both. But her father had never complained, she thought, a smile trembling on her lips.

As she turned away, uttering a wordless prayer for her father's safety and restoration to health, she noticed the exquisite clock which occupied pride of place on the mantelpiece.

Certainly Alain seemed in no hurry to return, she thought. Not that she wanted him to, of course, she hastily reminded herself, but, on the other hand, he could have made slightly more effort to ease her into her new environment. Didn't he realise how totally strange and isolated she must be feeling? she asked herself with faint resentment.

She tried to watch some television, but found it required more concentration than she was capable of. And a more extensive vocabulary too, she realised uneasily. She would probably have to have some intensive language coaching before she and Alain did any proper entertaining, although she could not imagine herself ever acting as hostess in these frankly formidable surroundings.

In spite of her new hairstyle and new dress, she was still a fish out of water. It was an oddly desolate thought, and her throat constricted suddenly.

Oh, no, she told herself determinedly. You're not going to cry. You're just tired and rather fraught after one hell of a day, so you'll go to bed—and, in the morning, you can start keeping your side of the bargain by getting to grips with this new life of yours.

She was on her way across the wide entrance hall when the telephone rang. For a moment she hesitated in case the Giscards reappeared from whatever fastness they had retired to and thought she was usurping their prerogative, but when its shrill summons went on and on unchecked, she reached out and gingerly lifted the receiver.

'Alain?' It was a woman's voice, low, warm and husky. *'C'est toi, mon coeur?'*

For a second, Philippa felt as if she'd been turned to stone. But what the hell was she surprised about? Alain had made no secret of his proclivities, after all. It was because of them that she was here at all. She just hadn't expected this kind of confrontation so soon.

She said curtly in French, 'I'm afraid Monsieur de Courcy is not here, *madame.*'

'And who are you?' Some of the warmth had dissipated.

'His wife,' said Philippa, and put down the phone.

CHAPTER THREE

PHILIPPA was shaking with temper, and another less easily defined emotion, when she closed her bedroom door behind her. If the phone rang again, it could burst into flames before she'd answer it, she told herself. Turning a blind eye to Alain's *amours*, as required, was one thing, taking messages from them quite another.

She stood still for a moment, taking a few deep breaths to restore her equilibrium. Madame Giscard must have unpacked for her, she realised, as she looked round her. Her toilet things were waiting for her, and one of the new nightgowns Monica had insisted on was lying, elegantly fanned out, across the turned-down bed.

Philippa looked at it with distaste. Its oyster satin and lace had cost more than she'd been used to paying for a whole term's clothes at art school, she thought with irritation. What a terrible waste of money for a garment no one would see but herself!

The bed itself came in for its fair share of disapproval too. She glanced at the draped and ruched green silk bedhead, and wondered if she would ever be able to sleep amid such opulence.

She shook herself mentally, telling herself she was now being petty. Maybe a warm bath would relax her a little.

The bathroom, needless to say, was the last word in luxury. Philippa, accustomed to fighting for her turn with half a dozen others, was in the seventh heaven as she lay back in the deep, scented water, feeling the tensions slowly seeping out of her.

She dried herself slowly on one of the enormous fluffy bath sheets, then experimented with some of the deliciously perfumed lotions and colognes provided before putting on the nightgown. She looked at herself judiciously in one of the long mirrors, and grimaced. The tiny lace bodice hugged her small high breasts, and each side of the sleek shimmering skirt was slashed, almost to the thigh. With her hair hanging, straight as rainwater, almost to her shoulders, she looked like a child playing at being an adult, she thought disparagingly.

She flicked the soft brown strands away from her face and walked back into the bedroom, halting with a gasp as she found herself face to face with Alain.

He looked almost as taken aback as she did herself, she realised, her face flaming.

He was still wearing the formal dark suit in which he'd been married, but he had discarded the jacket and silk tie, and unbuttoned his waistcoat.

'What are you doing here?' Her voice was husky with embarrassment as she looked round vainly for a robe, or some other covering to shield her from the totally arrested expression in his green eyes. 'What do you want? It's late.'

He said slowly, 'I came to wish you goodnight.'

'Well, now you've said it, perhaps you'll go.' Her tone was curt, and his dark brows lifted in surprise and hauteur.

'I also brought some champagne to drink to our future.' He indicated the ice bucket and glasses waiting on a convenient table.

'I don't think that's necessary.'

'But it's traditional—for a wedding night.'

'But it isn't—not really—I mean, we're not ...'
Philippa ground to a halt, her flush deepening. 'Oh,
you know what I mean.'

Alain poured wine into the glasses and held one out
to her. 'I am not sure that I do.'

She took the glass, holding it awkwardly. 'You said
that you'd—wait,' she reminded him, her voice trembling a little. 'That you'd give me time to—accustom
myself.'

He drank some champagne, watching her
meditatively over the rim of the glass. 'But how much
time, my reluctant bride? This year, next year, some
time—or never, perhaps?'

Philippa flicked her tongue round her dry lips. The
small nervous movement was not lost on him, she
realised, her nerves grating. 'I'll keep my word—when
it becomes necessary. But not yet.'

'And if I told you that it is necessary now—
tonight?'

'Then I wouldn't believe you.' Still holding her untouched glass, she took a step backwards. 'Please stop
saying these things, and leave me in peace as you
promised.' She paused, gathering her courage.
'Besides, you're obviously expected elsewhere.'

His dark brows snapped together. 'What is that
supposed to mean?'

'It means I'd be grateful if you'd ask your mistresses
not to telephone you here.' Philippa lifted her chin.
'Perhaps you should have warned the lady in question
that you're now, nominally, a married man. Get her
to ring you at your offices from now on. I'm sure
your secretary is used to dealing with such calls.'

There was a long and ominous silence. When he spoke, his voice was like ice. 'How dare you speak to me like that?'

'And how dare you expect me to act as go-between with your women?' Philippa spoke defiantly, but she felt frightened suddenly, wishing she hadn't mentioned it quite so precipitately. But she couldn't retract what she'd said now. 'Anyway, she's clearly waiting for you, so I wouldn't waste any more time.'

'When I want your advice on how to conduct my personal life, *ma femme*, I will ask for it.' There was a tiny muscle jumping beside his grim mouth. 'However, I have no intention of spending the night anywhere but here.'

There was another profound silence. Philippa swallowed. 'When you say "here",' she began. 'I hope you don't mean . . .'

He gave her a brief hard smile. 'I mean exactly what you think, *ma belle*.'

'No—oh, no!' She took another dismayed step away from him. 'You promised me . . .'

'Listen to me,' he said harshly. 'My first task when I left you earlier was to inform my uncle of our marriage. When he had managed to overcome his chagrin a little, he insisted that we dine with him tomorrow evening—so that he and his family may meet you, Philippa.' He shrugged. 'I could hardly refuse.'

'But he can't do that!' She gave him an imploring look. 'Please—you've got to put him off. It's too soon—I'm not ready to face anyone yet.'

'Exactly the point I am trying to make,' Alain drawled. 'They are expecting, my uncle, my aunt and my cousin Sidonie, to meet my loving and loved wife, not some frightened shrinking virgin. So we will need to present them with a normal marriage, not a pretence a child could see through. You begin now to see the necessity, perhaps?'

'No,' she said hoarsely. 'No, I don't. I can't meet them yet. You'll have to think of some excuse.'

'Au contraire,' Alain said quite gently, and put down his glass. The green eyes swept over her, making her feel, terrifyingly, as if the concealing satin no longer existed. 'I think I shall have to see what I can do to—persuade you.'

'Get out of my room.' Her voice cracked. 'Don't come near me—or I'll scream the place down!'

'Vraiment?' His brows lifted mockingly. 'And who do you imagine will hear you—or care? The Giscards are far too well trained to interfere.'

'You—bastard!'

'Calling me names will change nothing. We have a bargain, you and I. On my side at least it has been generously fulfilled, and will continue to be so, as long as I receive equal—generosity from you, *ma chère.'* He beckoned. 'Now, come here to me.'

'I'll see you in hell first! You gave your word—and you lied to me.' Panic was pounding in her chest, almost closing her throat. 'You can't do this! You don't even want me...'

'What,' Alain said softly, 'do you know of desire, *petite innocente*?'

'I know I don't want you.'

The words hung in the air between them. He gave her a long, considering look, then, without haste shrugged off his waistcoat and let it drop to the floor before beginning to unfasten the buttons of his shirt.

His lithe, muscular body was deeply tanned, his chest darkly shadowed with hair. Philippa watched him, petrified, hardly able to breathe as he began to unbuckle his belt. She'd seen men naked before in the life classes at art school, but Alain—this stranger she'd married—stripping in front of her like this was shockingly different.

He looked deep into the confusion in her hazel eyes. He said gently, almost mockingly, 'Shall I make you beg me to take you?'

She gave a cry like a small hunted animal, and threw the wine she was holding straight in his face.

He was very still for a moment, then he picked up his discarded shirt and dried the moisture from his face and chest, his eyes never leaving hers.

He said quietly, 'You should have more respect for good wine, *ma belle*. And more respect for me, also. I see I shall have to teach you.'

The glass dropped from her shaking hand and rolled away on the thick carpet as he came towards her. He took her by the shoulders and pulled her towards him, his fingers hard on her flesh, brooking no resistance. Then his mouth closed ruthlessly on hers.

When he'd kissed her before, he had been gentle. There'd been nothing to prepare her for this— onslaught. She tried to move her head, to escape from the suffocating pressure, but he would not allow that. One lean hand lifted to tangle in her hair and hold her still, while his kiss deepened, inevitably, inexorably.

He parted her lips with his, allowing his tongue to invade her mouth with devastating sensuality, plundering her warmth and sweetness with insolent mastery.

There was no point in fighting him—in struggling, Philippa realised from some whirling, fainting corner of her mind. He was too experienced, and more significantly, too determined. She was made aware once more of his physical power, the sheer muscularity of his body.

And her shocked consciousness told her that in these first brief moments, he was demonstrating to her with swift and frightening emphasis what passion could mean, and what other demands might be made of her before the night was over.

The heat of his hard body scorched through her thin nightgown, and even as she stiffened in helpless outrage she felt his other hand stroke down her body from the point of one shoulder to the curve of her hip, lingering on the way to shape her small, pointed breast in his palm.

She was not prepared for that, or for her body's shaken, helpless reaction to the first intimate caress it had ever received. She might hate him for what he was doing to her, but she couldn't control the hardening of her nipple under the subtle play of his fingers, or the swift onrush of moist heat through her whole body.

Then, his mouth still locked to hers, he lifted her and carried her to the bed. He placed her on the cool linen sheet and lay beside her. He stroked her cheek, turning her to face him so that he could kiss her again, slowly and explicitly, his hand travelling unhurriedly from her excited, tumescent breasts to explore with tantalising precision the exposed length of her silken thigh through the deep side-slit of her gown.

When he lifted himself away from her, she thought for one moment of agonised hope that he had relented, only to realise in the next second that he was simply removing the rest of his clothing. She turned away with a gasp to bury her heated face in the pillow.

She felt the slight dip of the mattress as he came to lie beside her again, and her whole body tensed, fear quivering through her, as his hand touched her shoulder.

'Relax,' he whispered. 'I'm not going to hurt you.'

'Another promise?' Philippa demanded bitterly, keeping her back rigidly turned to him.

'One I intend to keep.' His mouth touched the nape of her neck, blowing away the soft strands of hair to bare her skin for his caress. A shudder that had nothing to do with revulsion ran through her body.

She was not proof against this, she thought wretchedly, yet she had to be if she was to retain the least element of her self-respect.

He'd lied to her, broken a solemn promise, and she could not forgive him for that. If he wanted her, he would have to take her, she told herself bravely. Because she would not give, no matter what it might cost her.

When his hand began to slide the hem of her nightgown up towards her thigh, she stopped him with a little cry.

'Don't!'

'Then take it off for me.'

'No!'

'What is the problem?' Although she wasn't looking at him, she could hear the smile in his voice. 'You have some deformity that you've been keeping from me, *mignonne*?'

'You know quite well I haven't,' she said bitterly.

'How can I know?' he said. 'When I have only un-covered your body in my imagination—until now.'

Philippa, quivering with shame and indignation, found her nightgown deftly drawn over her head, and discarded on the floor beside the bed.

'Oh, God,' she said, half sobbing. 'At least put out the light.'

'No.' Gently but implacably he turned her to face him again. 'I want to see what my money has bought me.'

She closed her eyes, sinking her teeth into her lower lip as she endured his lingering scrutiny.

'What are you so afraid of?' he asked at last.

'I'm not afraid. I—I'm disgusted. I thought I could trust you, but you lied to me.'

He laughed softly. 'And now I'm going to lie with you, my little one. Why don't you stop fighting me in that stubborn mind of yours, and learn a little about yourself? Who knows? You might get a pleasant surprise.'

'Being betrayed and degraded hardly features on my list of enjoyable experiences,' she said raggedly.

'So you find my presence here with you a degradation.' His voice held a sudden chill. 'My profound regrets, *madame*. But it changes nothing. You can behave as childishly as you wish, but tonight you are going to learn what it means to be a woman. You might find it easier if you made a conscious effort to stop hating me,' he added drily.

'Never!' she said fiercely. 'I won't forgive you for this!'

His teeth glinted in a brief, unamused smile. *'Tant pis,'* he said, and began to kiss her again, his lips warmly, deliberately arousing as they moved on hers, then down the long line of her slender throat to her breasts.

The touch of his mouth, the stroke of his tongue against her flesh was a revelation—a pleasure that was almost pain.

I can't stand this, Philippa thought, as his lips delicately encircled each throbbing nipple in turn.

'Don't,' she said hoarsely. 'Just—do whatever it is you're going to do, then leave me in peace.'

'In my own good time, *mignonne*.' Alain's fingers feathered against her rounded thighs and lingered with persuasive purpose. 'Couldn't you defy your stern principles and meet me halfway?'

There was a new, almost disarming warmth in his voice. Philippa found herself shivering suddenly, tempted beyond all bearing to yield, to let him lead her down whatever sensuous path he wanted.

Her lashes lifted slowly, and she looked into the dark face so close to her own, registering just in time the flicker of amused triumph in the green eyes as he recognised her inner struggle.

It was the expression of a man, she thought dazedly, who was used to succeeding with women. The arrogant seducer who did not intend to fail with his—bargain basement bride.

She brought up her hand and slapped him across the face as hard as she could.

His head jerked back almost incredulously, then he swore under his breath, and his hands came down hard on her shoulders, pinning her to the bed.

She began to fight him in earnest then, her body struggling to be free of the weight of his, her hands flailing at him, nails clawing at his shoulders and chest.

He snatched at her wrists, pinioning them above her head, with one hand.

'Philippa.' There was a kind of anguish in his voice. 'In the name of God, no! Not like this, *je t'en prie*.'

'I hate you.' She hardly recognised her own voice. 'And I always will.'

He said harshly, 'So be it, then,' and parted her thighs without gentleness.

She cried out as he entered her, but it was more surprise than actual pain. In some crazy way, she wanted him to hurt her—wanted him to know the guilt of having torn her—made her bleed. But even in this she was thwarted.

Almost as soon as she'd registered that initial discomfort, it was over, and all she had as a focus for her anger and resentment was the bewildering unfamiliarity of what he was doing to her—the incredible sensation of his hardness and strength sheathed inside her.

She kept her eyes closed so tightly that bright dots began to dance behind her lids. She tried, in her head, to rehearse her nine times table, to remember poetry she had learned at school—anything that would stop her thinking about Alain, and the stark driving force of his body within hers.

But she couldn't remain totally impervious. She was only too aware of the graze of his sweat-dampened body on hers, and she could hear the urgent rasp of his breathing. In some strange way, that urgency seemed to be communicating itself to her. Deep in the centre of her being, in spite of herself, she could feel a spiral of dark, shamed excitement beginning slowly to uncoil...

A sound was torn from Alain's throat, harsh, almost agonised, then his body slumped against hers, shuddering in spasm after spasm as he buried his face in her breasts.

For a moment, she knew a disappointment, a yearning so intense that her body was nearly rent apart. Then she lay in utter stillness under his relaxed weight, while eternity seemed to pass.

At last, convinced that he had fallen asleep, she began slowly, and by degrees, to edge away from him.

Immediately, Alain's arms tightened around her. *'Qu'est-ce que tu as?'*

She said stiltedly, 'I'd like to get up. I want to go to the bathroom.'

Alain propped himself on one elbow and studied her for a long moment, his face cold and derisive.

'Why? So that you can wash all trace of me away from you?'

'Something like that.' Philippa bit her lip.

'I wonder if you can,' he said mockingly. 'But perhaps, my sweet bride, I don't want you to leave me so soon. Maybe, in a little while, I shall want you again.'

She stared up at the dark face above her, her eyes widening endlessly, and he laughed harshly.

'But again, perhaps not,' he said, and lifted himself away from her.

Philippa slid out of bed, grabbing at her discarded nightdress and huddling it on over her head. She was trembling violently, and her whole body ached in a totally alien way.

She was aware of Alain's gaze tracking her all the way to the bathroom, and was terrified that he might follow—might insist on forcing further intimacies on her.

Fortunately, the door bolted from the inside, and she slid the bolt into place, uncaring whether or not he heard it.

She dragged off her nightdress, hurling it on to the floor, then walked into the shower cubicle and turned on the hot spray, methodically soaping and rinsing every inch of her body, as she stood under the tingling jets of water.

Then she wrapped herself in a towel and sat down at the vanitory unit, staring at herself in the mirror.

With her wet hair plastered to her skull, she looked like a half-drowned kitten, her eyes enormous in her pale face. She lifted a corner of the towel and blotted some of the moisture from her face and neck, watching herself almost warily as if afraid she might break if she pressed too hard. She had heard, or perhaps read somewhere, that you could tell a woman's sexual knowledge from her eyes. But she could see nothing reflected in her own but pain and confusion.

She swallowed, noticing almost clinically that there were marks on her shoulders and breasts which would probably be bruises tomorrow. But then she bruised easily.

But not any more, she thought, lifting her chin. From now on, she would neither bruise nor break. She had become, through no choice of hers, Alain de Courcy's wife in every sense of the word. She knew now the worst that could happen to her, and, God help her, what she could expect from him in the future. She knew...

No one would ever say she looked untouched again.

It was a long time before she could force herself to go back to the bedroom, but when she did so, Alain had gone. She stood for a moment staring at the pretty, empty bed, with its dishevelled covers and tumbled pillows, then slid under the sheet, pulling it up to her neck. She turned out the lamp beside the bed, and lay in the darkness, curled up defensively, her arms clasped round her body.

The ache inside her had intensified, but what else, she thought bitterly, could she expect?

She had, after all, been violated.

She sank her teeth into her bottom lip until she tasted blood. All Alain's charm—all the consideration he'd shown her had been nothing but a façade. I am not a savage, he'd said that first evening in Lowden Square, but he'd lied. He was worse than that. He was a brute—an animal.

And you, said a small hard voice in her head. What about you? You threw wine at him, you hit him, you tried to scratch his eyes out. Is it really any wonder he reacted with anger? And you were angry too, not with him but yourself, because you'd actually started to enjoy what he was doing to you—you'd begun to want him—and your pride wouldn't allow that. So you fought him instead, and you lost.

Philippa moved restively in the bed, her head turning on the pillow in violent negation, as she tried to shut out the unwanted memories crowding back to torment her of Alain's mouth against her body—his hands...

No, she thought, it wasn't like that—it wasn't. He was vile—he forced me. I hate him for that, and I always will.

And as if in mockery of her unspoken words, she felt the fierce hardening of her nipples, and the swift tumultuous clench of her body in a need she'd never known existed until then.

With a groan, she rolled on to her stomach, burying her face in the pillow.

Damn him, she wailed silently. God damn him!

It was hours before she fell into a troubled sleep. When she woke, the small clock beside her bed told her it was past ten o'clock.

As she made to sit up, her bedroom door opened, and, as if programmed, Madame Giscard appeared with a tray.

'Oh, thank you,' Philippa said awkwardly in French, trying to use the sheet to conceal the fact that she was naked. 'I'm sorry if I've caused any inconvenience.'

The housekeeper gave her a look of polite astonishment. 'At your service, *madame*.'

She went to the wardrobe, selected a robe and brought it back to the bed, her face expressionless.

'Monsieur de Courcy left for the day some hours ago, *madame*. He asked me to tell you he will join you for lunch.'

Philippa thanked her again quietly, colour rising in her face, and watched her leave.

The woman's whole manner indicated that she was quite accustomed to serving breakfast in bed at all hours of the day to naked girls in Alain de Courcy's establishment. And the fact that he was legally married to the current occupant made no difference at all.

Philippa drank her chilled peach juice, and sampled the hot chocolate in its tall pot, and the crisp croissants wrapped in a napkin, without particular appetite.

During the wakeful hours before dawn, she had come to terms with the fact that she was caught in a trap of her own devising. However disastrous her marriage, she couldn't walk away from it as every fibre of her being was urging her to do, because otherwise the money for Gavin would cease. Alain had made that clear the previous night. So, somehow, she would have to get through the days—and endure the nights. Somehow.

She showered quickly and dressed in a well-cut russet skirt and a matching blouse. She was still very pale, and there were deep shadows under her eyes, but she made no attempt to disguise them with cosmetics. She looked, she supposed, shrugging, like any other girl on the morning after her wedding night—except that most brides probably looked radiant as well as exhausted.

It was a very long morning. Philippa soon discovered that her new environment ran like clockwork, needing no interference from her. In fact she was sure that any attempt to involve herself in Madame Giscard's superbly efficient régime would be strongly resented.

She wandered restlessly about the apartment, unable to settle. In spite of the stunning views over Paris from every window which she hadn't been conscious of the previous night, she still found it characterless, and wondered if she would ever feel at ease there.

But she couldn't spend the rest of her life looking at views. She would have to find some way of occupying herself—even if only to stop herself from thinking.

As lunchtime approached, she found herself becoming more and more on edge. The eventual sound of Alain's voice in the hall sent her scuttling to one of the sofas in the *salon*. She tucked her legs beneath her, pretending to leaf through a current affairs magazine, and hoping she looked composed and relaxed.

She heard him come into the room, and sat staring down at the picture spread on her lap until the photographs danced crazily in front of her.

'*Bonjour.*' As Alain broke the silence, she was forced to look up. She returned his greeting, annoyed to hear her own voice falter slightly.

'How was your morning?' He came to sit beside her on the satin-covered sofa, close, but not touching.

'Fine—and yours?' Was this how they were going to play it, she wondered hysterically, with meaningless social chit-chat?

'Busy.' He paused. 'May I offer you an aperitif?'

'Just some Perrier water—if there is some.'

'There can be whatever you wish,' he said politely.

Philippa sat clutching the glass he'd handed her. He had poured himself a large whisky, she noted before resuming his seat beside her, still at the same careful distance.

After a silence, he said, 'About last night . . .'

'I'd rather not talk about it.'

'I think we must.' His contradiction was courteous but implacable. 'My behaviour was quite unforgivable, after all. I can only offer you my profound regrets.'

His expression was as cool as his voice. Stealing a glance at him under her lashes, Philippa saw a faint mark on his cheek where one of her nails must have caught him.

She said stonily. 'It really doesn't matter. I—I married you, so I suppose I should have expected—

something of the sort.' She took a deep breath. 'You said you wanted a child. Well, perhaps it's happened—and you'll be able to—to leave me alone in future.'

Alain said curtly, 'I doubt, *ma femme*, whether matters generally arrange themselves quite so conveniently. However, let us hope you are right.' He swallowed the remainder of his whisky and sat for a moment, staring at the empty tumbler.

His face was expressionless, but Philippa was suddenly and frighteningly aware of an anger in him which transcended anything she had experienced the previous night—a violence that was almost tangible. She had the crazy feeling that at any moment, the delicate piece of crystal in his hand was going to shatter against the fireplace in a million glittering shards.

She made a little sound, and her hand lifted involuntarily to grab his arm. He glanced at her, and as swiftly and completely as if a wire had snapped, she felt the tension between them subside.

Alain set the tumbler down on a side table and rose to his feet. He gave her a smile which did not reach his eyes. 'Shall we go in to lunch now?'

Wordlessly she nodded, and together they left the *salon* and crossed the hall to the imposing dining-room, just as Madame Giscard was bringing in the soup.

The meal proceeded largely in silence. Philippa kept stealing covert glances at Alain across the flowers reflected in the sheen of the polished table. She had found to her cost last night how ruthless he could be. Now she had learned he had a temper too. She wondered what other discoveries the ensuing weeks, months—even years would unfold, and shivered inwardly.

'You haven't been eating,' Alain said brusquely, startling her. 'Is there something wrong with the food?'

'Oh, no,' she stammered. 'It's wonderful. I think I'm still rather tired . . .' She stopped abruptly, feeling the colour sweep into her face, and expecting some sardonic rejoinder.

But all he said was, 'Then have a rest this afternoon. You have to look radiant for this evening, remember.'

She kept her voice level. 'I'm hardly likely to forget in the circumstances.'

'That is unfortunately true. Last night was hardly a glorious hour—for either of us.' His smile was brief and tight-lipped. 'I shall try and behave with more consideration in the future. Tonight, for instance, will be enough of an ordeal for you, I think, without dreading my presence in your bed when we return. You have my word you will be left in peace and privacy.'

'Thank you,' Philippa returned uncertainly.

'And if you've finished your meal, you need not wait for me. Why not go and enjoy your siesta?'

She pushed back her chair, murmuring something incoherent in reply, and almost fled from the room.

She closed her bedroom door and leaned against it, staring at the bed, aware that she was breathing as rapidly as if she'd taken part in some marathon.

She was safe tonight, she thought, but that was the only guarantee she had. Some time, sooner or later, the door from the adjoining room would open, and she would be expected to submit to him—to allow herself to be used, for no better reason than that she'd been bought and paid for, and he wanted his money's worth.

There were tears suddenly, thick in her throat, and stinging her eyes.

She said aloud to the emptiness in the room, 'I don't think I can bear it.'

And knew before even the sound of her words had died away that she no longer had a choice.

CHAPTER FOUR

PHILIPPA was breathless with nerves as she sat beside Alain that evening in the chauffeur-driven limousine which sped them through the Paris streets to the suburbs where Louis de Courcy lived with his family.

The house was hidden behind a high wall. Craning her neck, Philippa could see only the tops of some elaborately ugly chimneys, as they waited for the electronically operated gates to admit them.

'My uncle has a phobia about thieves,' Alain muttered into her ear. 'He feels if he relaxes his vigilance even for a moment they may break in and steal his collection of tasteless porcelain, or ravish my cousin Sidonie. I think he over-estimates the desperation of such men.'

Philippa refused to laugh. With a hand that shook slightly, she smoothed a fold of the ankle-length jade green skirt she was wearing. The matching silk jersey top had a wide rounded neck and long sleeves, and she hoped it was all sufficiently formal for the evening ahead. Dressing for this unwanted dinner party had been rather like putting on a costume for a play where she was only the understudy, but expected nevertheless to go on and give a performance, knowing someone else's lines.

The clothes fit, she thought, as the car swept up the drive between depressingly formal flower beds. The girl doesn't.

The house itself looked square, solid and uncompromisingly dull. There were a number of other cars parked in the drive, and Alain cursed under his breath.

'So much for the quiet family dinner!' he said angrily. He turned to Philippa with a shrug. 'I'm sorry. I did not intend you to be subjected to this kind of occasion quite so soon.'

Philippa lifted her chin. 'I'll try not to speak out of turn or use the wrong cutlery,' she assured him shortly, and his mouth tightened.

'That is not what I meant, and you know it.'

The door was opened by a manservant in a white jacket, who gave them a stately greeting and told them that Monsieur and Madame were waiting in the *salon* with their other guests.

'Are we the last to arrive, Gaston?' Alain made a last-minute adjustment to his tie.

'By no means, *monsieur*,' he was assured, as Gaston conducted them along an elaborately decorated hallway.

Alain clasped Philippa's icy fingers in his. *'Courage, ma belle,'* he whispered as Gaston threw open the double doors of the *salon* and announced them.

All conversation in the room ceased abruptly. Philippa seemed suddenly to be the cynosure for a hundred pairs of eyes. She straightened her shoulders, feeling a faint blush warm her face. At second glance, she could see that the room actually held at most twenty people, one of whom was advancing to meet her.

Louis de Courcy was not tall, and was inclined to rotundity. He was slightly bald, and wore a neatly trimmed beard. His fleshy lips beamed welcome, but his smile did not reach his eyes, which were as dark as polished agate, and as hard.

He bowed over Philippa's hand. 'My new niece,' he said. 'But what a delight! And how cruel of Alain to have kept you from us. As his only living relatives, we might have expected to attend his wedding.' He spread pudgy hands dramatically. 'To be informed only after the event was a blow—I will not conceal it.'

Philippa was embarrassed, but she had been primed by Alain.

'I'm afraid my father's poor health dictated that the ceremony be as quiet and private as possible, *monsieur*.'

'So quiet, indeed, that none of my friends in London had any idea it had taken place, or was even intended,' Louis de Courcy said, still smiling. He turned, beckoning. 'Joséphine, allow me to present Alain's bride to you. Sidonie, come and greet your cousin.'

Madame de Courcy, who was built on the same lines as her husband, showed no great enthusiasm for the encounter. Her plump fingers just touched Philippa's, and then she made way for her daughter.

Philippa's first thought was that Sidonie de Courcy was almost exactly as Alain had so unkindly described her. She had a pale, unhealthy skin, pitted with acne scars, and her hair looked coarse and without lustre. She too was overweight, and her cream dress accentuated this, fitting too snugly over her bust and hips. Her smile at Philippa barely curved the corners of her mouth, but when she turned to Alain there was a transformation.

'You look well, *mon cousin*.' Her flush was not unbecoming. 'Clearly marriage agrees with you.'

Oh, dear, Philippa thought. She's in love with him and hurting. I didn't bargain for this.

Louis de Courcy cut in urbanely, 'You must allow me, Alain, to present your bride to these few friends who have gathered to meet her. This is, after all, a great day for our family.'

And a nightmare for me, Philippa thought, as she was led round the circle. It was all very formal and correct, and she smiled politely until the corners of her mouth began to ache. Louis de Courcy performed the introductions in English. She was aware that she was being patronised, and resented it. Her French, culled from her wanderings with Gavin, was far superior to the usual schoolgirl variety. However, it gave her an advantage in that she could translate for herself the whispered comments which followed her round the circle. She understood that she was 'very young, very English'—'*un peu gauche*'—and, more tellingly, with a note of real malice, 'She will be no match for Marie-Laure, *ma chère*.'

Her heart lurched, but her smile didn't falter. Marie-Laure, she thought. Presumably the woman in the scandal. Well, at least, now, she had a name to attach to that sultry voice on the telephone.

She had just completed the round of introductions when the door of the *salon* opened again, and Gaston ushered in the last arrivals, a man tall and distinguished-looking with grey hair and a moustache, and a much younger woman, blonde and very beautiful, the voluptuous magnificence of her figure set off by the daring chic of her expensive black dress.

'Monsieur le Baron de Somerville-Resnais,' Gaston announced into a sudden, profound silence. 'Madame la Baronne de Somerville-Resnais.'

The room wasn't just quiet, Philippa realised. It was alive with tension, and a kind of excited expectancy that was almost tangible. She had the feeling that everyone present was holding his or her breath. She looked uncertainly across at Alain, who was standing at a small distance from her. For a moment she thought he'd been turned to stone. She saw too that he was very pale except for an angry flush along his cheekbones. Her heart thudding, she began to wonder.

Louis de Courcy was hurrying forward, smiling expansively, his hands outstretched in welcome. 'Ah, *mon ami*, what a pleasure that you and your charming wife could join us! This is a joyous occasion, you understand. We are celebrating the marriage of my nephew Alain to a charming young girl from England. Allow me to present her.'

Philippa was aware that Alain had come to her side. His face was impassive now, but as he took her hand in his and led her forward Philippa could feel the rage in him, dark and powerful as an electric current, communicating itself through the touch of his flesh on hers.

This woman—this Baronne was Alain's mistress. This was Marie-Laure, she thought, nausea rising in her throat.

And Alain's uncle had deliberately contrived this situation to embarrass them all—had invited the Baronne and her husband to come here tonight to force a confrontation, to reactivate all the gossip and

rumour that their marriage had been supposed to
defuse. To damage Alain all over again.

The Baron was drawing himself up in outrage, his
face glacial. He said, 'My dear de Courcy, this is a
family occasion on which Marie-Laure and I should
not intrude. Permit us to withdraw and leave you to
your—celebration.'

Which of course was exactly what Louis de Courcy
wanted, Philippa realised in a flash. He had engineered
it so that the Baron would leave in a jealous huff,
causing a whole new scandal, giving him a whole new
range of ammunition to fire at that crucial board
meeting.

She walked forward, smiling, holding out her hand.
She said in perfect French, 'Oh, please don't go,
monsieur. I'm having such a wonderful party, and it
would spoil it if you—if anyone left. I would feel it
was all my fault.' She let her voice become girlishly
excited. 'Besides, there's going to be champagne!
Surely you'll stay and drink to my happiness?'

The Baron paused, his narrowed gaze flickering
between Philippa and Alain. At last he said, 'Who
could resist such a charming invitation, *madame*? We
will stay, naturally, and drink to your—health. Come,
Marie-Laure.' He drew his wife's arm possessively
through his and led her away.

As the Baronne passed, Philippa was aware of a
drift of some exotic, musky scent, and the sweep of
a pair of deeply lashed violet eyes, assessing and dis-
missing her in one comprehensive glance. Marie-Laure
de Somerville-Resnais shared, it seemed, the consensus
of opinion that between Philippa and herself it would
be no contest.

A shaft of anger scored through Philippa, mixed with another emotion less easy to define. Presumably Alain had discussed his marriage with his mistress, told her the terms on which it was based. But that did not mean she merited the other woman's contempt, she told herself roundly. Who was Marie-Laure to judge—to criticise? On what terms had she herself married the Baron, who looked old enough to be her father?

It was a relief when Gaston announced dinner. It was a long and tedious meal. Philippa, on edge, supposed the food was good, but tasted little of it. She wanted to talk to Alain—to warn him that their sham marriage hadn't fooled anyone for a moment—but he was at the other end of the table.

'Do tell us, my dear,' Joséphine de Courcy leaned forward, her eyes unwinking as pebbles. 'You and dear Alain—such a romance—and so quick too! Quite fascinating. And the question we all wish to ask is— how did you meet?'

Philippa, grimly aware that she was once more the centre of attention, forced a light smile. 'Was it really quick? I feel as if I've known Alain forever. We met through my father, actually. He's Gavin Roscoe, the landscape painter, and Alain bought one of his pictures—*The Bridge at Montascaux.*'

There was an astonished silence. Philippa stole a look at Alain, whose whole attention appeared to be centred on the peach he was cutting into quarters.

'So you are an artist's daughter,' Louis de Courcy said jovially at last. 'Perhaps you will introduce a note of much-needed culture into our crude commercial world.' He laughed heartily, and was echoed by an

uneasy ripple of amusement round the table. 'Do you
share your father's interest in painting, *ma chère*?'

'His interest, perhaps, but little of his talent,
although I was actually at art school when Alain and
I decided to marry,' Philippa returned composedly.
'In fact,' she added with sudden inspiration, 'I plan
to continue my studies here in Paris with—Zak
Gordano.'

'I am impressed,' Louis de Courcy said slowly.
'Monsieur Gordano has a formidable reputation as a
teacher.'

Philippa shrugged. 'Then I hope I can persuade him
to take me as a pupil.'

'I do not think you need concern yourself on that
score,' Sidonie said rudely. 'As Madame de Courcy,
you will find all doors open to you.'

'Not Zak's,' Philippa told her coolly. 'Painting is
what matters to him, not social standing.' Although
the fact that he's a friend of my father's might help,
she added silently, as she leaned back in her chair.

'Your wife, nephew, is clearly a woman of talent,'
remarked Louis.

'Each day I spend with her brings some new and
delightful surprise,' Alain said smoothly.

Philippa shot him a glance under her lashes. His
face revealed little, but she felt that delight was hardly
his predominant emotion at her impulsive
announcement.

At the conclusion of dinner, the whole party
adjourned to the *salon*. Conversation was desultory.
Everyone seemed to have accepted that the promised
sensation was not going to take place after all. The
Baron and his wife were the first to leave, and not

long after that Alain announced that he and Philippa were also departing.

'So soon?' his uncle queried. 'We are desolate.'

'And my wife and I are on our honeymoon,' Alain returned evenly. 'I am sure the company will understand, and forgive us.'

They were in the limousine, travelling back towards the apartment, before Philippa could begin to relax.

'That,' she said with feeling, 'was a truly ghastly evening.'

'Which you handled with great aplomb. Please accept my thanks.' Alain paused. 'You understood at once, of course, why my uncle invited us there tonight?'

'It was fairly obvious.' Philippa drew a breath which ached in her chest. 'She's very beautiful—Madame de Somerville-Resnais.'

'Yes.' The flat monosyllable told her nothing, and it was too dark in the car for her to read his expression with any accuracy. He volunteered no other comment, and after a moment or two Philippa sighed soundlessly and settled back in her seat, resigning herself to a silent journey.

When they reached the apartment, Alain excused himself with abstracted politeness and went to speak to the Giscards. Philippa made straight for her room. The tensions of the evening had given her a slight headache, which the journey home had done little to alleviate.

Alain obviously had a great deal on his mind, she acknowledged, as she took off the jade green top and skirt, and began to remove her make-up. It must have been traumatic for him to be suddenly confronted by his mistress and her husband, quite apart from the possibility of an ugly scene. The sight of her must have revived all kinds of memories for him too, and made their enforced separation doubly bitter.

As far as she was aware, Alain and the lovely Baronne had not exchanged as much as a private glance, let alone a word, unless they communicated in some secret lovers' code. But presumably they both intended the affair to continue at some time in the future.

But Alain would have to be careful, she thought. The Baron was clearly a jealous and suspicious man, who would not hesitate, if provoked, to revenge himself in a very public way. And next time she might not be there to retrieve the situation.

She gave a mental shrug. From now on that was Alain's problem, and he would have to deal with it. All she wanted to was lie down and sleep for eternity. Her siesta that afternoon had been little more than a restless doze punctuated by some frankly disturbing dreams. Try as she might, she had not been able to prevent memories—images from the previous night filtering into her consciousness. Or maybe she hadn't really wanted to forget...

Her heart missed a sudden, startled beat and she swallowed, strangling the traitorous thought at birth. Of course it couldn't be that, she chided herself, as she unfastened her suspenders. She was just too tired to think rationally, that was all.

She was standing in her ivory silk teddy, with one foot perched on the dressing stool, as she tried to slide off a gossamer stocking, when there was a brief tap at her door, and Alain walked in.

He halted at once, his brows lifting in surprise, touched by amusement, as he assimilated her state of undress.

'*Mille pardons,*' he murmured, his mouth curving with a totally sensual awareness as he regarded the unknowing provocation of her pose.

Blushing to the roots of her hair, Philippa hurriedly regained her balance, snatching up a robe in pale lemon shirred cotton and fastening it round her.

'Do you have to barge in like that?' she asked resentfully.

He shrugged. 'I did not think you would have begun to undress so soon. And I wish to talk to you. Do you question my right to do so?'

'No,' she said in a low voice. 'But can't it wait until morning? I'm rather tired. I found the evening a strain...'

'I can only apologise for my uncle.' His voice was grim. 'He will go to any lengths, it seems, to embarrass and discredit me. Only this time, thanks to you, his scheme did not work.'

'But it might next time.' Philippa picked up a brush and began to stroke it over her hair. She did not look at Alain. 'We—we haven't fooled anyone, you know. They don't believe in our marriage. Everyone knows that your affair with the Baronne is still going on.'

'How clever of them,' Alain said bitingly. 'Then you and I, *mignonne*, will have to find a way to convince them that they are in error.' The words hung in a loaded silence. Then he said abruptly. 'What did you mean about resuming your art studies?'

'Exactly what I said.' She decided not to tell him that she had thought of it on the spur of the moment.

Let him think it was a considered decision. 'My father always wanted me to study with Zak Gordano.'

'And what about my wishes in all this? Have you considered them at all?'

'Why should it bother you if I start painting again?' Philippa stared at him, her hand stilling.

'It might be better to—postpone your plans for a while. To concentrate your energies instead on learning to be my wife, perhaps?'

Sudden colour flared in Philippa's face. She hurried into words. 'That's hardly going to fill my days. Your apartment is run like clockwork, and your other houses, I expect. I can't imagine the Giscards want my interference.'

'That is not precisely what I meant. There are other elements to our relationship, after all, besides housekeeping.'

Philippa was silent for a moment, then she said quietly, 'I thought I'd learned all I need to know about—*that* too.'

'Oh, no, *chérie*.' Alain's voice was silky. 'You are not that naïve.' He walked to her side and took the brush from her nerveless fingers, tossing it on to the dressing-table. His hand closed round hers, his thumb rubbing lightly, cajolingly over the inside of her wrist. 'Lovemaking is also an art, my wife, and your lessons in love are only just beginning.'

Her pulses were going mad suddenly, fluttering, throbbing unevenly, and she was aware of each and every one of them.

She snatched her hand away. 'I think you're confusing love with sex, *monsieur*,' she said huskily. 'And may I also remind you that you promised to leave me in peace tonight?'

There was a smile in his voice. 'You did me a great service, Philippa, when you persuaded Henri to stay at the party. Am I not even allowed to thank you with a kiss?'

She shook her head. 'We made a bargain,' she said stiltedly. 'I was just—keeping my side of it, that's all.'

There was the barest pause, then he said, 'Just as you wish. I hope, however, that you will seriously reconsider your plans to start painting again.'

'No.' She lifted her chin. 'My mind is made up. I need something—some kind of life for myself. After all, I'm not your prisoner.'

'I cannot imagine a cage that would hold you,' he said with faint acid. 'You mean, then, to defy my wishes?'

'When they're as unreasonable as that—certainly.' She paused. 'I don't interfere with your—hobbies. I think you should allow me the same courtesy.'

There was another taut silence.

'I think,' Alain said slowly, at last, 'that I should have had a vow of obedience included in our marriage ceremony.'

'Which I would have refused to take,' Philippa retorted crisply.

'Then it's *impasse*.' He shrugged, sounding amused. 'Very well, *ma femme*. Join your art class, if that's what you want, but do not allow your painting to interfere with your social duties. I shall be entertaining various members of the board of De Courcy International over the next week or two, and I expect you at my side, my devoted and docile wife,' he added with irony. 'Do I make myself clear?'

'As crystal,' she nodded. 'I won't let you down.'

'No,' he said. 'You will not. Our marriage must convince everyone.' His voice was thoughtful, and the green eyes travelled over her from head to foot in a devastatingly sensuous assessment. He lifted a hand and very gently traced the outline of her cheek, pushing back the soft strands of hair as he did so. He said quietly, 'Are you sure, *mignonne*—quite sure that you wish to spend the night alone after all?'

She tried to speak, but her mind suddenly seemed to have stopped functioning. He was standing too close to her, she thought dizzily. His voice alone was a seduction, quite apart from the way he was looking at her—the smile in his eyes . . .

She was aware of a hot, unfamiliar excitement, drying her mouth, and sending a wild, secret trembling through her body. She found herself wondering crazily what it would be like to go into his arms of her own free will—to give without restraint all he might ask of her. And in return to know everything . . .

As Marie-Laure already knew . . .

The thought invaded her consciousness like an icy deluge, shattering the spell which held her enclosed, and sending her reeling back to a kind of sanity, as the exact events of the past twenty-four hours came relentlessly into focus.

It was Marie-Laure he wanted, of course. He'd had the torment that evening of seeing his mistress, but knowing that she was denied to him, so now he was turning instead to the girl he had made his partner in the most cynical marriage bargain of all time. Because she was female, after all, and available, and he could use her for an hour to two to find a temporary sexual oblivion. Because that was the most it could ever be, and she needed to remember it.

And I, Philippa thought shakily, I might have allowed that. I might have let my curiosity lead me into a complete betrayal of myself and my principles. Because for me it might not have ended there. It might instead have been a beginning . . .

Her mind closed, in rejection and fear.

She heard herself saying softly and stonily, 'I wish to be left in peace, as you promised. I'm not a substitute for your mistress, Alain.'

He was very still suddenly, looking at her, the laughter, the beguiling tenderness dying from his face.

'I need no such reminder,' he said bleakly, at last. 'You hardly resemble her, after all.'

She supposed the gibe was deserved, but pain lanced through her just the same. Last night, he had seemed to find her desirable, but compared with Marie-Laure's sensual, voluptuous beauty, she could see she had very little to offer, except perhaps a certain novelty value.

'Before I leave you to your precious peace, my dear wife,' his voice stung, 'I should tell you the main reason I came here tonight was to inform you that I have telephoned the clinic, and your father's condition is stable. It is too soon to know whether the treatment is having any effect, but his doctors wish you to know they are optimistic.'

Philippa stared down at the carpet, her eyes blurring. She told herself it was a relief. 'Thank you.' Her tone was subdued.

'*Pas du tout,*' Alain said too politely. 'It is useful, perhaps, to remember precisely why we are together at this moment. And also why it would be foolish to expect any more from each other than the terms of our agreement.'

'Very foolish.' It was an effort to keep her voice
steady.

'So now we both know where we stand, *madame*.'
His voice sent a shiver along the length of her spine.
'But understand this. Our bargain will be kept, and
you will take care how you challenge me in future. I
do not need any spoken vow to make you obey me, and
I shall not hesitate to enforce your obedience, in
the privacy of this room as well as in public, if I think
it necessary. There is too much at stake.'

Philippa leaned back against the dressing-table, her
fingers gripping the carved edge, her heart slamming
against her rib cage.

She said thickly, 'I won't forget.'

Alain sent her a swift, hard smile. 'Good. Then I
wish you a pleasant night.'

She watched him walk away from her across the
room. Heard the door close behind him.

No, she thought, she would not forget. She would
never forget. She had been granted a temporary
reprieve, that was all. Because there was no escape
clause in the contract she'd made with Alain de
Courcy. And she would have to live with the consequences. All of them.

She stared across the room at the bed, and her whole
body began to tremble.

CHAPTER FIVE

ZAK GORDANO stood back, hands on hips, head on one side. For a long moment he said nothing, and Philippa held her breath. Then he nodded.

'That's not bad,' he said. 'It's not good either, but it's an improvement on anything you've produced so far.'

Philippa's grin lit up the world. 'That,' she said, 'is the nicest thing anyone's ever said to me.'

Zak raised bushy eyebrows. 'And you only married—what is it—a month ago?'

'Six weeks,' Philippa corrected, her expression suddenly wooden.

'So long?' Zak mocked. 'My God, no wonder the honeymoon's over and the pretty speeches are finished!'

She had to smile in spite of herself. 'Yes—well, do you really think my work's getting better?'

'Maybe.' Zak paused, fingering his beard, his dark eyes studying her closely. 'The thing I keep asking myself is—why do you want to do this? God knows you don't need to paint. You're married to a millionaire. No question about where your next meal is coming from.'

Philippa's eyes went frowningly to the canvas on the easel. 'Is that a problem?'

'There's certainly something,' Zak spread his hands. 'What can I say? You're too locked up in yourself—too inhibited to paint as you should be doing. You're still feeling your way, instead of going for broke. Holding back all the time. So I ask again—why bother?'

She looked troubled. 'Am I wasting my time—and yours too? Is this what you're trying to tell me?'

'Hell, no. If I thought that, I'd have said so on day one.'

Philippa was silent for a moment, then she said slowly, 'I suppose there could be several reasons why I'm doing this. I need to establish an identity for myself—to prove that I exist as a person in my own right, not just as a well-dressed adjunct to Alain. That's—not always easy to remember.'

She paused. 'And there's Dad, of course. He always wanted me to paint. I feel I'm keeping faith with him somehow. That when I'm struggling to get the paint on the canvas here in Paris, I'm helping him fight for his health over in New York. Does that sound utterly ridiculous?'

'It doesn't sound ridiculous at all,' Zak told her gently. He paused again. 'What's the latest news on Gavin, anyway?'

She grimaced. 'Slow. I call the clinic every other day. They tell me it's still too early for any definite prognosis, but that everything's going to plan. I just keep hoping.'

'That's as much as any of us can do.' Soberly Zak patted her shoulder. 'Tell me, Madame de Courcy, what does Gavin think of his son-in-law?'

Philippa swallowed. 'Well, they don't really know each other very well as yet,' she evaded.

Zak nodded. 'One of these days I'd be real interested to hear the history of this marriage of yours, and so would Sylvie. She says you haven't got the look in your eyes which means happiness for a woman. Yet your husband's a good-looking guy, and definitely no slouch when it comes to women, or so Sylvie says.'

Philippa shrugged. 'I think most marriages have to go through a period of adjustment,' she countered.

'And that's what yours is doing?'

'I think so. Tell Sylvie to stop worrying about me.'

'I will. At the same time, I'll tell the sun not to rise tomorrow.' Zak paused again. 'Speaking of my wife, she's making bouillabaisse tonight. Says there's enough for you too.'

'Oh, Zak, I can't.' Regretfully Philippa shook her head. 'I have another dinner party to go to—a business affair. I'd much rather be staying for Sylvie's bouillabaisse.'

'Some other time, then,' said Zak. 'See you tomorrow, honey.'

Philippa was thoughtful as she walked slowly down the narrow staircase that led from the studio to street level. Even she could see that her work was still too tentative. She wondered if it was Alain's attitude that was colouring her approach. His disapproval of her decision to resume her studies was still patent, if unvoiced.

Yet he had nothing to complain about, she told herself defensively. She was keeping her side of the bargain to the letter. Whenever he required her to be at his side, she was there, groomed and smiling. She was beginning to be less shy too, and could hold her own in conversation. And Alain played his part too— she could not deny that. He was attentive and affectionate, every word, every gesture expressing his pride in her, and his satisfaction with her as a wife.

She was becoming used to hearing herself described as *'charmante'*, and no one, to her knowledge, had drawn any more unfavourable comparisons with any other woman. So in that way, at least, he had reason to be pleased with her.

She bit her lip. But that, of course, wasn't all. If their marriage could have been lived totally in public, it might have counted as a success. It was when they were alone together that it all went wrong. Oh, they didn't quarrel, or anything like that, she acknowledged glumly. It might almost have been preferable if there had been a few rows. In fact there were times when she found herself deliberately provoking Alain—trying to get a reaction. But all to no avail.

No, Alain was invariably courteous to her, even charming in an aloof way, and his behaviour didn't alter one iota on the rare occasions he came to her bedroom.

She felt her face warm. She didn't really want to contemplate those brief, embarrassing encounters in the darkness. Those swift, almost clinical couplings which were all she was called on to endure.

She supposed she should be thankful for the consideration he invariably showed her. At least there were no more troublous attempts to seduce her. But gratitude, she had discovered, was not always the uppermost emotion in her mind, as she lay, tense and trembling, in his arms. She was aware of a strange restiveness when he left her, an aching void deep inside her.

She told herself it was resentment. He might have a legal right to use her body, but that didn't mean she had to like it. Besides, resentment—endurance, also represented safety. They enabled her to retreat from

Alain emotionally behind the barrier they offered—to resist the temptation of his physical attraction which still tormented her. Because she couldn't afford to relax her guard against him, even for a moment. The strange hunger in her body told her that, and she was disgusted at her own weakness.

And what part Marie-Laure de Somerville-Resnais still played in his life, she could only guess. Certainly there were nights when he did not return to the apartment. He offered no explanation, and she certainly never asked for one. He knew the risks implicit in such a relationship, after all, she told herself stonily.

The threat of the emergency board meeting, with its attendant vote of censure, had been withdrawn, at least temporarily. Louis de Courcy had been forced to acknowledge that his campaign to overthrow his nephew as chairman had been weakened by his new respectability as a married man. But that did not mean he wouldn't still be watching and waiting for Alain to make some mistake, some slight slip. And a resumption of his affair, however discreet, with the beautiful Baronne would be exactly the excuse that his uncle was looking for, Philippa thought, biting her lip. As for herself, her own feelings on the subject—well, that side of Alain's life was none of her business, was it?

The irony of it all was the overt envy she sensed from most of the women she met. They clearly imagined she lived a life, not just of luxury, but also of blissful fulfilment.

If they only knew, she thought, with a little sigh as she emerged into the late afternoon sunlight.

The men seemed to come from nowhere—two of
them, scrawny and greasy-haired, dressed in denims.
One of them pushed her, sending her flying to the
pavement, while the other one grabbed at her
shoulder-bag.

Philippa screamed, clutching at the strap, and
heard, somewhere near at hand, another male voice
answer.

Suddenly the grip on her bag was released, as the
two muggers took to their heels and vanished around
the corner.

'Are you hurt, *mademoiselle*?' Hands helped
Philippa gently to her feet, then set about retrieving
her coin purse, compact and other belongings which
had become strewn across the pavement in the
struggle.

'No, I'm fine.' The knees of her jeans were torn,
and her skin was grazed. She would have bruises
tomorrow, she thought, as she leaned against the wall,
trying to recover her breath, and taking her first look
at her rescuer.

He was young, dark-haired and undeniably
attractive. He was smiling, but his face was concerned as he handed over her bag.

'But you have had a shock, yes? There is a little
bar in the next street. You must have some coffee—
a cognac. Yes, I insist.'

She was glad to take the arm he offered. When she
tried to move, she found her legs had turned to jelly.
The bar was only a hundred yards away. He seated
her at a pavement table, and summoned a waiter with
a flick of his fingers. The coffee and brandy arrived
with the speed of light.

'That's better, *hein*?' he asked as she sipped.

'Much better. I'm so grateful, Monsieur...?' Philippa hesitated, the question in her voice.

'I am Fabrice de Thiéry, entirely at your service, *mademoiselle*.' His eyes were warm, flickering over her with that appreciation which was so totally French.

She flushed. 'Actually, it's *madame*. My name is Philippa de Courcy.'

He looked startled, then his expression changed to regret. 'You look altogether too young to be a married woman.' His gesture indicated her casual clothing.

'I study art—I work in a studio just back there. The street has always seemed so quiet. I never imagined...'

'Of course not. Probably they have been watching you—hoped to take you by surprise.'

'I can't imagine why,' she said candidly. 'I had nothing of real value in my bag. I only ever carry a few francs at the most.'

'When one has nothing, *madame*, a few francs can seem a great deal.' He smiled at her. 'Tell me about your painting.'

Her blush deepened. 'Oh, it's just something I do for the time being. Are you interested in art?'

'I am interested in most things,' he said. 'But I work in accountancy.' He leaned forward. 'You look sad. Did they hurt you, perhaps, more than you have said?'

Philippa shook her head. 'No—it's just that—well, my husband doesn't really approve of my painting, and now that this has happened, he'll insist on my using the car and the chauffeur, and that's the end of my independence.'

'And that matters to you?'

'Very much.' She forced a rueful smile. 'The thieves stole more than they realised.' She set down her coffee-cup and looked at her watch, an exclamation escaping her. 'Oh, look at the time! I'm going to be late. I must find a taxi...'

'I have a car. May I drop you somewhere?'

Philippa hesitated. 'I don't like to impose,' she protested. 'You've been so kind already...'

He pooh-poohed that. 'Anyone would have done the same,' he declared, signalling for the bill. 'What is your address?'

She told him, and his brows rose almost comically. 'Oh, *lá, lá.* You are the wife of *that* de Courcy?'

She nodded. 'Does that mean I don't get my lift?'

'Of course not. But your husband is right.' He was frowning. 'You should not be walking the streets of Paris unescorted. But I will take you home straight away, and perhaps he will not be too angry, *hein*?'

'I have to thank you again for rescuing me,' Philippa said, as his car drew up outside the apartment building.

'It was my pleasure.' He took the hand she held out to him, and kissed it. His eyes smiled at her. 'But I still think you look too young to be married,' he murmured. '*Au revoir*, Madame de Courcy.'

'*Au revoir*, Monsieur de Thiéry.' As she scrambled out of the car, Philippa was aware her heart was thumping. How pleasant it was to be regarded as attractive and not merely useful, she thought, as she rode up in the lift. When she got to the door, she realised to her dismay that her keys were not in her bag.

They must have fallen out, and I missed them when I was picking everything up, she thought, as she pressed the buzzer.

Madame Giscard answered the door, wearing her usual grim expression. 'Monsieur has been asking for you,' she began, then her eyes widened. 'But what has happened, *madame*? Your clothes are torn, and there is blood!'

'Someone tried to snatch my bag, but fortunately they were disturbed.' Philippa tried to shrug it off. 'I'm sorry if Monsieur Alain is waiting. I'll get ready straight away.'

She dashed to her room, took the cream brocade skirt and the jacket with the deeply squared neckline from her wardrobe, grabbed some underwear and flew into the bathroom for a hasty shower.

She was back in her bedroom, clad only in her white silk and lace bra and briefs, frantically applying her make-up, when the door opened without ceremony to admit Alain.

'What is this Henriette has been telling me? That you've been robbed?' His voice was sharp. 'How did it happen?'

Philippa sighed. Now the recriminations would start, she thought.

'I'd just come out of Zak's,' she told him. 'These two men tried to grab my bag, then another man appeared and they ran off. They didn't actually manage to take anything,' she added appeasingly.

Alain's brows rose. 'They cannot have been very determined thieves if the presence of one other man put them to flight,' he said, after a pause. 'How fortunate that he happened to be there.'

'Yes, it was,' Philippa agreed fervently. 'He was marvellous afterwards as well—bought me a drink, and then drove me home.'

'Ah.' Alain strolled over to the window and glanced down into the street. 'And do you know the name of your gallant rescuer?'

'Of course. He's called Fabrice de Thiéry.'

'I must try and trace him—offer him some reward.'

'If you want—but I don't think he expects anything. He was just—very kind.'

Philippa winced slightly as she turned to pick up the brocade suit. She'd washed her grazes in the shower, but they still stung.

'You are hurt?' He came to her side, frowning.

'I fell over.' She shrugged. 'It's nothing.'

'Hardly nothing.' He pushed her down on to the edge of the bed and knelt in front of her examining the marks on her leg.

'Honestly, it's all right.' She felt vulnerable— embarrassed as his hand gently cupped the back of her knee.

'Have you applied some antiseptic? Should you use a plaster?'

'They're only a few scratches. They're not even bleeding any more.' Philippa moved restively. 'Alain— please. I need to finish getting ready. We're going to be late.'

'There is no hurry.' His voice was husky. '*Pauvre petite.* This should not have happened.' He bent his head and touched his mouth, swiftly, sensuously to the angry mark on her knee.

Longing, sharp and bitter and totally involuntary, pierced her to the core of her being. A shocked gasp at her own reaction rose to her lips and was suppressed. She moved restively, but his hand detained her.

'Don't pull away.' There was sudden anger in his voice. 'Is it just my touch you find so abhorrent, or did you flinch from this stranger also?'

Her voice was uneven. 'It—isn't the same thing. He was just being—kind.'

'And is that what you want from a man, my innocent one—just—kindness?' His fingers moved gently on her skin, making it spark and tingle in response.

'I don't know,' she said rawly, stifling a sob. 'Alain, let me go—please!'

'But perhaps it does not please me.' He looked up at her gravely. 'Maybe there is nothing between us that pleases me, or you either, my cool, prim little bride.' He kissed her again, his lips gentling her knee before travelling up to her slender rounded thigh. His mouth was warm and lingered, as if savouring the fragrance of her skin. His hand began to stroke her, questing along the lacy rim of her briefs, almost touching her intimately, but not quite—yet, at the same time, making every secret crevice of her body clench in longing.

Philippa's head fell back. Suddenly it was difficult to breathe—to think. And impossible to speak, to utter the protest that should—that must be made.

In one lithe, fluent movement Alain rose from his knees and sat beside her on the bed, his breath warm on her cheek.

'Is there other damage?' he asked softly. He took her hands, making her extend her arms, so that he could study their bare length. Then he pressed his lips to the delicate skin inside each elbow in turn, before allowing the caress to travel unhurriedly down to her wrists.

'There's—nothing.' She hardly recognised her own voice. The beat of her pulses seemed to vibrate through her body, filling the world. He must be aware of their haste, their flurry. Must be...

'That, *ma belle*, I intend to discover for myself.' His voice was a whisper. His fingertips skimmed her shoulders in a featherlight caress that sent every nerve-ending tingling. He slid down the straps of her bra, then his hands began a leisurely descent to find and release the fastener and allow the tiny garment to fall away from her body completely.

His fingers cupped her breasts, stroking the tautening nipples lightly and rhythmically until they stood proud and erect.

'No,' he said softly, his mouth curving in appreciation of her helpless physical response to his touch. 'They are still unflawed—perfect.'

He drew her forward without effort into his arms, holding her across his body, looking down into her face, his eyes unsmiling—questioning. Then he bent to her, and his lips parted hers in a demand that would not be denied.

Philippa felt her body melt into surrender. Alain lifted her against him so that the excited rosy peaks of her breasts were brushing the starched frills of his shirt. He deepened the kiss, making her taste him—drink from him, as he did from her. Of her own volition, her small hands slid upwards and clasped his neck, holding him close.

They seemed to be enclosed in a golden, honeyed silence, broken only by the fever of their own breathing.

The knock on the bedroom door, swift and respectful though it was, seemed like a hammerblow, shattering the fragility of their enraptured world in a second.

'Monsieur Alain—Madame!' It was Madame Giscard's voice. 'Marcel wishes me to say that the car is at the door.'

'Oh, my God!' Philippa, jolted back to stark reality, struggled to free herself from Alain's arms. A few yards away, her dressing-table mirror provided a merciless reflection of herself, almost naked, flushed with desire and surrender. 'Let me go—you must...'

'Must I?' The green eyes glittered down at her. 'Why don't I tell Marcel and the car to go to the devil, and spend the evening here with you, *chérie*?'

'Because we're expected at this dinner party.' Her voice shook uncontrollably, and every inch of her body seemed to be blushing as she dived to retrieve her bra, and the modicum of modesty it represented. 'You can't afford to offend people, Alain,' she gabbled on, as she covered herself. 'You're not out of the wood yet. Your uncle Louis is just looking for an excuse...'

'I think,' Alain cut across her, his face icily sardonic, 'I think that my uncle Louis is not alone in that.' He rose, walked across to the dressing-table and stood for a moment, smoothing his dishevelled hair, and straightening his tie. 'I shall await you in the *salon, madame.*'

Left to herself, Philippa struggled into her clothes, fumbling with buttons and zips with unwontedly clumsy fingers.

Hastily she renewed her lipstick, and ran a comb through her hair, letting it swing simply into place around her hectically flushed face. She stood for a moment, staring at herself in the mirror, almost unable to believe what had happened.

If it hadn't been for that knock on the door, she thought, she could have made a terrible—an irretrievable mistake. It made her cringe to think how easily Alain had engineered her surrender—how close he had come to subjugating her completely.

She shivered as she picked up her cream kid purse. She would need to be even more on her guard from now on, she told herself as she went to join him in the *salon*.

The party was being held at a large house outside Paris. It was a warm evening, and the doors on to the terrace had been left open, so that the other guests, who were mainly much older than either Alain or Philippa, could enjoy their aperitifs overlooking the formal gardens, if they wished.

Philippa was thankful to be able to make her escape into the fresh air. She had been tautly aware of Alain's enigmatic gaze fixed on her during the car journey, and although little had been said, she knew, with a kind of desperation, that the encounter between them had been merely interrupted, and not terminated completely. Now that she had unwittingly betrayed her own needs, her own capacity for response, she knew that Alain would no longer be content with the embarrassed passivity she had shown in his arms up to now.

She was unable to explain how she could have been so weak—such a fool. The shock of the attempted robbery must have temporarily lowered her resistance, she thought wretchedly, as she leaned on the stone balustrade, holding her untouched glass of *kir royale*.

And now Alain was stalking her—the hunter who knows his victim is helpless, and is poised for the ultimate victory. The kill.

She grimaced slightly, knowing that she was being overdramatic. Yet wouldn't it be a kind of death to yield to Alain, to allow herself to become his plaything for a few hours, and then to see him walk away in search of other amusement when he tired of her?

Her whole body seemed to constrict sharply and painfully. That was something she couldn't permit—couldn't even contemplate. Because for her there could be no casual giving. Once she belonged to Alain, he would have her heart and soul in his uncaring, predatory hands. And that would be total disaster.

She lifted her chin. Well, she would not be his victim. Nor would she be his toy—to be used because he was bored with the outward respectability which marriage had forced upon him, and thought it would be entertaining to seduce his unwilling wife.

'Ah, Madame de Courcy, I have been looking everywhere for you.' Her hostess's smiling tones reached Philippa's ear. Smothering a sigh, she prepared for yet another introduction.

'May I present one of our oldest friends, Monsieur Gérard de Crecy? Unfortunately, Madame his wife has succumbed to *la grippe*, so he is accompanied by his daughter, who says you are already acquainted.'

There was a trace of a musky scent in the air. As she turned obediently, her polite smile already in place, Philippa became aware of it. Recognised it.

She hardly noticed the portly white-haired man who was bowing to her, and murmuring a courteous greeting. Her eyes were fixed on the woman at his side, clad in a clinging gown of midnight blue.

'Madame de Courcy.' The full lips were smiling, but the violet eyes glittered with malice. 'I hope so very much that you remember me?' said Marie-Laure de Somerville-Resnais.

CHAPTER SIX

PHILIPPA'S lips parted in a soundless gasp. At the same time, the glass she was holding slipped from her grasp and shattered on the flagstones at her feet, splashing its contents on to her cream brocade skirt as it did so.

Her hostess, exclaiming in distress, waved away Philippa's confused apologies, decreeing that the skirt must be sponged before the *crème de cassis* in the drink stained it irretrievably. She would summon her housekeeper, who was a treasure, and would know the correct way to achieve this.

The last thing Philippa was aware of as she was led away by the housekeeper was Marie-Laure's smile, feline and triumphant. And, as she passed him in the doorway, Alain's thunderous expression.

Waiting in a cotton wrap, while her skirt was attended to, she fumed inwardly at her own *gaucherie*. She'd behaved like an idiot, as Alain would undoubtedly tell her later. All she'd needed to do was smile coolly in acknowledgement of the other woman's presence, then ignore her.

At the same time she acquitted their hosts, Monsieur and Madame le Grès, of engineering another confrontation between Marie-Laure and herself. They were kindly souls, friends of Alain's late parents, as well as business colleagues, and heavily involved in charity work. They probably didn't even know that there was any involvement between Alain and Marie-Laure. And, of course, the Baronne's father was quite within his rights to ask his daughter to accompany him to a formal dinner if his wife was ill.

No, it was just one of those unfortunate coincidences, and now her stupidly over-the-top reaction to Marie-Laure's presence could easily have set all the tongues wagging again, she thought miserably.

Her skirt was eventually returned to her, miraculously restored, if a little damp in places, and she was able to join the rest of the party as they went into the dining-room. She was immediately besieged by concern and goodwill.

Her husband had explained the terrible incident that had befallen her earlier that day. To be robbed in the open street—*quelle horreur*! Such lawlessness! It was no wonder that she was *affreusement nerveuse*. But how was it that she should be in the street alone?

'I was just leaving my painting class,' Philippa explained lamely. 'I work at a studio every day. I wasn't expecting anything to happen.'

'Ah, yes, your little career as an artist.' Marie-Laure leaned forward, her expression solicitous. 'It still continues? You have not yet wearied of it?'

'I'm not likely to do that,' Philippa said crisply. 'It's too important to me.'

Marie-Laure shrugged creamy shoulders. 'You mean there is some lack in your life, for which you seek compensation?' Her brows rose in simulated amazement. 'How can it be possible? I hope that our dear Alain is not failing in his duties as a husband.'

There was a sudden shocked silence, and a number of eyebrows were raised in earnest. Madame le Grès hurried to fill the breach with a description of the plans the local community were formulating to celebrate Bastille Day, and conversation became general again.

Philippa sat back in her chair, her heart thumping. Alain was at the opposite end of the dining-table, and she did not dare look at him. What on earth was the Baronne trying to do? she asked herself in bewilderment. Her remarks had been indiscreet to say the least. It was almost as if she was deliberately trying to make trouble, stir up more gossip. Yet, surely, it was in her interests too that there shouldn't be any more scandal. So what was going on?

She had to force herself to eat her dinner and chat brightly to her neighbours, behaving as if everything was perfectly normal. With any luck, Marie-Laure's comments would be simply written off as a sample of female spite, and not attended to too closely, she told herself without particular conviction.

Afterwards, in the *salon*, coffee was served, and music was played, as a background to conversation. Philippa made sure she was always one of a group well away from Marie-Laure's vicinity.

Although I'm being perfectly ridiculous, she told herself. By avoiding her like this, I'm putting myself on the defensive, and giving her an advantage. I should let her see that I'm indifferent to her—and impervious to her little poisoned darts. The trouble is, I keep remembering that woman's remark that I'm 'no match for Marie-Laure' and believing it.

It seemed a very long evening, and she was too on edge to really enjoy talking to the people around her, although they couldn't have been kinder. But they still wanted to hear about the attempted robbery, and she would have preferred to forget about it. She felt suddenly oppressed by the noise of laughter and chatter, and stifled by the cigarette smoke mingled with expensive perfume which filled the room.

She needed to be on her own for a few moments, preferably in fresh air. The doors on to the terrace had been closed during dinner, but one of them was slightly ajar, and Philippa slipped unobtrusively through it into the darkness beyond.

She stood perfectly still for a moment, drawing deep, grateful breaths of the cool, flower-scented air into her lungs. She realised almost at once that she wasn't alone. From the other end of the terrace she glimpsed movement in the shadows and heard the mutter of lowered voices.

With a faint grimace, she half turned to go back indoors.

'Alain.' The name came to her on a throaty, seductive whisper, impossible to ignore or forget. Philippa's head came round sharply, and she peered through the gloom to the far corner of the terrace where a trellis network interwoven with climbing plants provided a screen. Then, almost as if it had been summoned, the moon emerged from behind a cloud and she saw them, standing locked together, Marie-Laure's arms round his neck, her body straining passionately against his.

'Alain, *mon amour.*'

She didn't want to see any more—hear any more. Only a few hours earlier that might have been herself, she thought, pain slashing at her, as she turned, fumbling her way blindly back into the *salon*. At least she'd been spared that, if nothing else.

Perhaps it wasn't just a coincidence that Marie-Laure was here tonight. Perhaps she and Alain had planned it that way, so that they could meet, snatch a few illicit moments together. They'd been clever about it. She hadn't noticed either of them leave the room, and nor, she could swear, had anyone else. It was a pleasant evening, and a good party. They were all too involved, too interested in their own conversations, which was what the lovers had probably relied on.

And this time, contrary to popular belief, the wife had been the first—indeed, the only one, to find out.

Not that it was strictly true, because she'd always known. That was why Alain had married her, for God's sake. She was—camouflage. Only—seeing them together had made it all too real somehow. Had fixed her with an image of desire, of passion and sheer sensual urgency that she would never be able to forget.

A maid approached, offering more coffee, and she took a cup, swallowing a mouthful of the powerful black brew, feeling it scald against her aching throat.

'Philippa.' She jumped as Alain appeared suddenly at her side, his hand closing on her arm.

His face was grim as he looked down at her. 'It was you—just now on the terrace?' As she nodded mutely, he said harshly, half under his breath, 'I thought so.' He glanced round him. 'We need to talk, you and I. I'll find Madame le Grès and tell her that we're leaving.'

'No, thank you.' She freed herself, gently and with dignity. 'I don't want to leave yet. I—I'm enjoying myself,' she added defiantly. 'And I have no intention of spilling another drink, or making a fool of myself in any way, so please don't worry about me.'

'Do you think I care about that?' he said harshly. 'I have to talk to you in private—to explain.'

'You explained when we met.' Philippa stared down at her coffee cup as if it was the most amazing and imaginative artefact known to the world of man. 'It's all right, Alain. You're paying me very generously to provide a cover-up, and turn a blind eye to your— diversions. That's what I'll go on doing.' She swallowed past the lump in her throat. 'But I will not— *not* provide one of those diversions myself. In future I'd like my bedroom door to be provided with a lock and a key.'

The silence between them tingled in her brain, beat on her eardrums.

Eventually Alain said coolly and courteously, '*D'accord, madame.* It shall be exactly as you wish.'

'And there's one more thing.' She continued to look down at her coffee. 'I don't think anyone here noticed you were missing—but it isn't very wise to take chances like this, particularly when Madame de Somerville-Resnais focused attention on us all once this evening already.'

'I am grateful for your advice, *madame.*' His tone was frozen silk. 'But, under the circumstances, Madame de Somerville-Resnais, and my relationship with her, need no longer be any concern of yours.'

'I understand,' Philippa said, and turned away.

But it wasn't true. The realisation that she didn't understand—didn't accept—struck her with all the force of a thunderbolt. Brought her to a standstill, coffee-cup in hand.

In fact, she understood only that she wanted to burst into tears, to scream and stamp her feet, and howl her misery to the four winds. She wanted to hurl the remains of her coffee over Alain's immaculate dress shirt, and scratch her nails down his face until she drew blood.

And then she wanted to find Marie-Laure and... She drew a shuddering breath. It was better to stop right there.

The power, the enormity of everything she was feeling almost overwhelmed her. As did the implications of it all.

Jealousy, she thought. That's what I'm feeling. I'm jealous. But I can't be, because that would mean that I wanted Alain for myself. Maybe, even, that I'd fallen in love with him. And that's impossible. It can't be true.

Because if it is true, what can I do? How can I bear it?

She squared her shoulders. She thought forcefully, I won't let it be true.

'Pardon, madame?' The look of smiling incomprehension from someone standing near her told her that she had inadvertently made that last avowal aloud.

Like an automaton, Philippa laughed, apologised, let herself be drawn into the conversation, absorbed into the group.

And all the time, pounding in her head like a steam hammer, came the silent despairing plea, Dear God, don't let it be true. Don't let me love Alain. Please don't let me love him.

She could only hope, forlornly, that her prayer would be answered.

'What the hell's the matter with you today?' Zak demanded in exasperation. He pointed at Philippa's drawing board. 'The assignment was meant to be a simple one. I wanted you to draw the lady on the dais—just a representation of the nude human form. Since when have you decided to go in for Cubism?'

Philippa flushed. 'I haven't. It's just—well, life-drawing has never been my strong point.'

'You can say that again!' Zak stared at her drawing and groaned. 'According to this, Jeannine looks as if she has about ten major bone deformities. It's probably actionable.' He turned to the model who was stretching cramped muscles and reaching for her wrap. 'You don't want to see this, *chérie*. It will only upset you.'

Jeannine smiled placidly, and went away to change with a wave of her hand.

Zak gave Philippa a measuring look. 'So what's the problem? Yesterday's wallet hijack? They say lightning never strikes twice in the same place.'

Philippa smiled stiltedly. 'I hope not. No, I just have things on my mind.'

'Gavin, I suppose. Honey, what can I say? You've just got to trust the doctors. You won't improve his condition in New York by fretting over it in Paris.'

'I know.' Philippa was guiltily, miserably aware that she hadn't given her father a thought in twenty-four hours. 'I'm sorry, Zak. Today's been rather a waste of time, hasn't it?'

'You've had better.' Zak took the drawing board and put it down somewhere else. 'Go home, Philippa. Try and relax. Get that good-looking husband of yours to take you out to dinner.' He leered at her. 'Just for starters, that is.'

Philippa flushed. 'He's probably—busy.'

'Then tell him to relax as well,' Zak said largely. 'I want you here tomorrow ready to do some real work.'

Easier said than done, Philippa thought gloomily as she walked downstairs. The previous evening she had driven home with Alain in a frozen silence. He had wished her a curt goodnight and gone to his room, leaving her to tell herself over and over again that was exactly—precisely what she'd wanted.

She went on saying it at intervals during a long and restless night. At some time before dawn, she had conceded defeat, got up, and crept barefoot to Alain's room. It was empty, the bed unruffled and unslept in. She'd stared at it for a long time, then returned soundlessly to her own room, and wept.

The locksmith had arrived to attend to her bedroom door almost before she had finished breakfast that morning. Madame Giscard had worn an expression of outrage as she supervised his endeavours. Philippa was not sure she blamed her.

The housekeeper had also informed her glacially that Marcel would be available to drive her to and from her art class. The orders were from Monsieur Alain.

She came out into the street and looked for the car, but it wasn't waiting for her. Small wonder, she thought, glancing at her watch. She was a good hour earlier than usual.

'Madame de Courcy.' She turned, alarmed, in time to see Fabrice de Thiéry loping towards her across the road.

'I hope you didn't think I was another thief.' His smile warmed her. 'I wanted to see you to return these.' He produced her key ring from his pocket and held it out to her. 'I must have picked it up by mistake yesterday.'

'Oh, thank you. What a relief! I hadn't dared confess I'd lost them.'

'Your husband is such a monster?' He sounded amused, but his eyes were serious.

'No—no, on the contrary,' Philippa said hastily. There was a pause.

Then, 'You are early today,' he remarked. 'I was lucky to catch you.'

'Not really.' Philippa sighed. 'I have to wait in future to be driven home.'

'Well, that is the sensible course.'

'Yes, but it isn't what I wanted.'

He looked at his watch. 'You have time, perhaps, for another coffee?'

Philippa hesitated. The sensible course in this instance would be to decline gracefully, and she knew it.

'You're going to refuse, aren't you?' Fabrice de Thiéry said ruefully. 'Well, I don't blame you. Your husband is a formidable man, after all. He would not wish you to make a friend of someone of such little importance as myself.'

Philippa stared at him. 'Is that what you really think?'

'But of course.' He looked slightly embarrassed. 'After I left you, I made some enquiries. If it had not been for the keys, I don't think I would have dared approach you again.'

Philippa lifted her chin. 'Monsieur de Thiéry, I would be delighted to have coffee with you.'

She learned a considerable amount about him in the half-hour that followed. She discovered that his parents lived in Rouen, where his father had a printing business, and that he was an only child. Fabrice was working in Paris, completing his training in accountancy with an international firm. In the winter he played rugby, and he enjoyed Japanese films. The information poured out of him.

It was very pleasant, Philippa realised, to sit in the sunlight with someone who so obviously found her attractive. And if a warning voice in her mind murmured that this was a situation fraught with potential pitfalls, she chose to ignore it. And if Alain disapproved of her new acquaintance, what did it matter? she asked herself defiantly. He was hardly in any position to criticise, after what she had seen on the terrace the night before. She was simply having an innocent cup of coffee at a pavement café, so what did he have to complain about? She wasn't embarking on a love affair.

All the same, the glow of admiration in Fabrice's eyes, the way he leaned towards her, and almost touched her hand, yet didn't quite—these things were balm to the inner wounds which Alain had inflicted. It humiliated her to remember how she'd clung to him—how she'd allowed him to kiss her—touch her. The way she'd almost forgotten that he was only playing some cynical game with her, amusing himself for a few hours, even though his heart, mind and body belonged to another woman.

She sighed inwardly when she thought of Marie-Laure. Yes, she was beautiful, with a body that would be any man's fantasy. But Philippa found herself wishing that she liked her more, or thought she was worthy of Alain's obsession with her. Was he so besotted that he couldn't see how spoiled and spiteful she was, or did he just not care?

'All of a sudden,' Fabrice said softly, 'I feel I am talking to myself.'

Philippa snapped out of her brief reverie with a start. 'I'm sorry—that was rude of me.' She drank the remainder of her coffee. 'I have a lot on my mind, you see.'

He nodded gravely. 'I do understand. I know more than you think, perhaps.'

She laughed, reaching for her bag. 'After two cups of coffee? I doubt it.'

'I know for example that you are not happy,' he said. 'That your husband lives a life totally his own.'

Philippa bit her lip. 'I'm not prepared to discuss my marriage with you, or anyone, *monsieur*.'

'Now I have made you angry!' He groaned. 'I apologise. It is not my place to judge.' He put out his hand and touched her fingers. 'Please say you forgive me and that one day soon you will drink coffee with me again?'

This, Philippa knew, was the moment to back away. To smile politely, and make some non-committal reply. She was married, and she shouldn't be making assignations with another man, however innocuous. And if I was really Alain's wife, she thought with a pang, I wouldn't even be contemplating such a thing. But as it is . . .

'What are you thinking? That it might make your husband angry to know that you sit in the sun and talk—and smile a little?'

'Why should he mind?' she said coolly. 'I live my own life too.'

'Then I may see you again? I have to ask, you understand, because I have nothing else belonging to you that I can use as an excuse.'

Philippa stared at him, her eyes widening. 'Do you mean you deliberately kept my keys?' she asked slowly. 'That was very wrong ōf you, *monsieur.*'

He nodded. His smile was rueful and appealing. 'Forgive me? I know it was wrong, but I could not bear just to see you walk out of my life. We will meet here tomorrow at the same time?'

'Perhaps,' she said. 'I don't know.'

His hand closed round hers. 'I shall wait until you come,' he said. '*A bientôt*, Philippa.'

'*Au revoir*, Fabrice.' Her smile was shy, uncertain, as she withdrew her hand.

He was nice, she told herself defensively, as she walked back towards Zak's studio where the car would be waiting. She liked him, and it would be pleasant to have a friend—someone to compensate for the loneliness of her life.

With her painting, and Fabrice for a friend, maybe her sham of a marriage wouldn't hurt quite so much any more. Perhaps she would even learn in time to tolerate Marie-Laure's presence in her life.

As she turned the corner, she wondered suddenly if Alain would be equally tolerant about Fabrice. He had no right to be otherwise, of course, considering his own conduct, but she knew he would be perfectly capable of operating a double standard.

But I'm not contemplating an affair, Philippa told herself with decision. I don't want to be involved— not with Fabrice, or Alain either.

Her throat closed painfully at the thought, and her hands clenched into fists at her sides.

I don't want to be hurt again, she went on silently. Or to spend any more sleepless nights crying. No, I just want to sit in the sun, and talk—and smile a little.

Surely there's no harm in that, is there?

Suddenly, in her mind, she saw Alain's face etched in lines of harshness, his green eyes glittering with anger as they'd been the previous evening. And she shivered, remembering the ruthlessness of his response when she had provoked him before, on their wedding night.

No matter how innocent her intentions, she thought, as she crossed the street to the car, she would have to be very careful. Alain de Courcy was not a man to cross.

CHAPTER SEVEN

'I CAN'T,' Philippa said. 'It's impossible, and you know it.'

Fabrice took her hand and held it firmly. 'But why not? It is a concert, nothing more. The music of Ravel and Debussy, whom you have told me you enjoy. Why should you not be my guest?'

Philippa sighed. 'Fabrice,' she said gently, 'I've told you a dozen times already—I'm a married woman.'

'And will attending a concert break your marriage vows?' he asked tartly. '*Mon Dieu*, Philippa, your husband has no such scruples, I assure you.'

Philippa stiffened defensively. 'I don't know what you mean.'

Fabrice shook his head. 'This crazy loyalty of yours,' he muttered. 'He does not deserve it, Philippa. You must know that. The man is notorious. His *affaires* are blatant. Why, even as we speak together...'

'You mustn't talk about Alain like that,' Philippa said forcibly, as pain lanced through her. 'If you persist—well, I shan't be able to meet you again.'

'Don't say that.' Fabrice's clasp on her hand tightened. 'These few snatched moments together have become my life. You cannot take them from me.'

'And you shouldn't say things like that either.' Philippa, her face warming, tugged her fingers free of his grasp. 'You promised to be my friend, Fabrice.'

'Then let me as a friend escort you to this concert,' he said promptly, forcing a reluctant laugh from her.

'Oh, you're incorrigible!'

She was beginning to find his increasing possessiveness an embarrassment, yet, she had to admit, his company had been a lifeline to her also over the past weeks, in view of the continuing breach between Alain and herself.

She bit her lip. The lock she had demanded on her bedroom door had been fitted, but it had proved totally unnecessary. Since their quarrel, Alain had not been anywhere near her room on any pretext whatsoever.

In fact, he had been away from Paris a great deal, ostensibly on business, although there had been many times, lying awake, staring into the darkness, when she had wondered...

When he was at home, their only encounters seemed to be at the meal table, and the social events to which he still insisted she accompany him, and where he continued to play the part of the attentive, devoted husband.

Clearly, she thought wanly, you can fool some of the people most of the time. And her awkward reception of his attentions was, even more surprisingly, attributed to the natural shyness of a newly married girl, and smiled on approvingly.

At the apartment, Philippa felt increasingly that she was living on a knife-edge of tension. Alain's behaviour to her was always courteous, but totally aloof. Even when he stood next to her when they were out together, and, on rare occasions, touched her, she felt the complete impersonality of the contact, and it chilled her. However physically close they might appear to onlookers, she knew that in reality they were light years apart.

Which was why she had turned with a kind of relief to Fabrice, and the undemanding companionship that, at first, he had seemed to offer.

But of course, she supposed ruefully, she had been naïve to think that state of affairs could continue indefinitely. Fabrice wasn't some kind of escort service but a young normal attractive man. And now their relationship seemed to be fast approaching a point of no return, and she wasn't sure how she felt about that.

The question she had to ask herself was—no matter what Alain's conduct might be, did she really and truly want to have an affair with Fabrice or anyone else?

And the instinctive answer which invariably presented itself was a resounding no.

So it simply wasn't fair to Fabrice to keep him hanging around hoping, when she knew perfectly well there was nothing to hope for. There was no future in their relationship, and without doubt she ought to tell him so, quite unequivocally.

But, although she knew it was selfish, she was reluctant to give Fabrice his marching orders. The fact was he at least represented a little human warmth and contact in the increasingly bleak desert of her life. Zak and Sylvie were wonderful, of course, but seeing them together, observing at first hand the close fabric of their marriage, and comparing it with the empty shell she herself inhabited, was becoming almost unbearable.

Her work, she knew, was becoming increasingly superficial and trivial. Zak was having to criticise her over purely fundamental things, and she could tell he was worried about her.

'You need to commit more of yourself, honey,' he told her over and over again. 'It would do you good

to get away on your own somewhere for a few weeks—
a few months even—and paint yourself into ex-
haustion. Let whatever's going on in that mixed-up
subconscious of yours take over. Find out what you're
about.'

She'd smiled and said it sounded a wonderful idea
but it was impossible now. Maybe some time in the
future . . .

Her commitment, after all, she told herself, was to
being Madame de Courcy, and not some voyage of
self-discovery which might or might not be successful.

But one thing she knew about herself was that if
she could roll back time, and find herself once more
in the library at Lowden Square, she would run a
million miles from Alain rather than submit herself
to the pain of this pretence of a marriage.

And the fact that he hadn't deceived her about his
way of life, and she'd gone into the arrangement with
her eyes wide open, made no difference at all—
provided not the slightest consolation.

Her only real concern at the time had been Gavin,
and the precious lifeline that Alain seemed to offer.
She'd given little thought to her own needs and
emotions, living in close proximity to someone of
Alain's attraction. She should have considered the
implications, her own sexual naïveté and vulner-
ability included, before agreeing to his terms.

Yes, she had been desperate, as he'd pointed out,
but if she could have foreseen the desolation that
awaited her as his non-wife, then she knew she would
have reneged on the deal—told him to find someone
else.

But it was too late now, and at least she had the
consolation of knowing that Gavin's condition had

taken a decided upswing. The clinic had managed to isolate and identify the mysterious virus which had attacked him, and there had been no further deterioration or wastage. In fact, her father had even regained a certain amount of mobility in his right hand and side. It was restricted, but it was there, and for that she was deeply, tearfully thankful.

It didn't make her marriage to Alain the right thing to have done, necessarily, but it helped her justify the desperate measures that she had undertaken, and tell herself that if Gavin's health and vigour were going to be restored, then this present pain was worth suffering.

'Philippa?' Fabrice's voice reproached her, drawing her back from her reverie. 'Where have you been? You haven't been listening to a word I've said!'

'I'm sorry,' she apologised. 'I was thinking about my father.'

'Your father?' His face was crestfallen.

She realised she had dented his ego a little and hastened to make amends. 'I'll consider going to the concert, Fabrice, I promise.'

He beamed at her. 'That's wonderful! And you'll tell me your decision tomorrow, *hein*?'

'Don't rush me.' She forced a smile in return.

'I would never do that.' He shook his head. 'It is just that I cannot bear to see you so unhappy and trying to be brave. Don't you deserve some happiness—to be the centre of a man's life—to be loved?'

The emotionalism in his voice disturbed her. He'd never spoken this frankly before, she thought. These were deep waters they were getting into.

She glanced at her watch. 'I really have to go. Marcel will be waiting, and it's getting difficult to find excuses why I'm not always waiting for him outside the studio.'

'And you are afraid he will tell your husband?' As she pushed her chair back, Fabrice rose too, his expression challenging. 'Why should he care? When he meets with his beautiful Baronne, Philippa, it is not just to drink coffee, I promise you.'

She bent her head. 'I—suppose not,' she agreed stiltedly. 'But all the same, I have to go. *Au revoir*, Fabrice. *A demain.*'

She slung her bag over her shoulder and walked down the street quickly towards the studio. She was stricken to find that the identity of Alain's mistress was apparently common knowledge outside the circle in which they moved. This was exactly what we were trying to avoid, she thought, dismayed. What on earth could Alain be thinking of? Or was he now so obsessed with the beautiful Marie-Laure that he'd ceased to think altogether? That he'd decided his mistress was worth the possible loss of his company after all? Because he'd provided his uncle with the perfect weapon to use against him.

She glanced at her watch again, and slowed her footsteps. For once she was much too early for Marcel, but not far away there was a square with a small parade of galleries and boutiques which she'd always meant to visit. She could kill some time there.

She was standing looking critically at an abstract canvas which occupied one gallery window in glorious isolation, when a voice behind her said without particular pleasure, 'So it is you. I thought so.'

Philippa started slightly and turned to meet the unfriendly gaze of Sidonie de Courcy.

'Hello,' she returned politely, concealing her dismay. 'I didn't realise you were interested in abstract painting.'

'I'm not,' Sidonie said, shrugging. 'But there is a shop near here where I buy some of my clothes. Is that what you are doing—shopping?'

The question seemed so pointed that Philippa wondered if by some mischance Sidonie had seen her with Fabrice.

'Why, no,' she said coolly. 'I've been at the studio, painting. The session finished early today.'

'Ah, yes,' Sidonie said with faint derision, 'your art lessons. Well, if they amuse you, what harm is there? And you will need something to do with yourself, after all, when Alain divorces you.'

Philippa's fingers tightened painfully on the strap of her bag, but she kept her face impassive.

'Is Alain planning to divorce me?' she asked lightly. 'He hasn't mentioned it to me.'

'You mean you didn't know that the Baron de Somerville-Resnais has had a heart attack, and is seriously ill? In fact, he is not expected to live longer than this week.' Sidonie's eyes widened in well-simulated surprise. 'But perhaps Alain has kept the news from you—out of compassion. It cannot be very nice for you to have to live with the knowledge that you have just been used as a stopgap. Of course, when the poor Baron dies, and you are no longer required as a decoy, it will be a different matter. Everyone is asking how long Marie-Laure will pretend to be the grieving widow.'

She gave a little giggle. 'Poor Alain, how angry he must be! He has gone to all the trouble of marrying you, and now he must face the inconvenience of a divorce, when, if he had only waited a few little weeks, Marie-Laure would have been free anyway. Everyone finds the situation *fort amusante*, you understand.'

'I can well believe it.' With a superhuman effort, Philippa crushed down the nausea which threatened to overwhelm her. 'It would obviously solve a lot of problems if I also had a heart attack—and just faded out of the picture.'

Sidonie giggled again. 'Oh, I do not think Alain would expect you to go to those lengths, I am sure if you simply agree to the divorce, and don't make trouble for him, you will find him more than generous.'

Philippa's heart was beating slowly and painfully, thudding against her ribcage.

'In that case, I have nothing at all to worry about.' She made herself smile at Sidonie. 'I hope your shopping is successful.' She let her eyes travel over Sidonie's unbecoming outfit of a beige coat and skirt, teamed with a saffron-yellow camisole. 'But if you'll take my advice, you'll try a different boutique altogether,' she added, and walked away, leaving Sidonie gazing after her with an expression of baffled rage.

Philippa rounded the corner, then stopped, leaning against the wall for a moment. She was shaking all over, and her legs felt like jelly. Waves of anger, mingled with desolation, were buffeting her.

Was this really what Alain intended? To dismiss her with a generous pay-off so that he could marry Marie-Laure after the usual decent interval—whatever that meant? Her nails dug sharply into the palms of her hands.

It was true he'd seemed even more abstracted lately, but in view of their rift Philippa had hesitated to ask if anything in particular was troubling him.

She closed her eyes. According to Sidonie, everyone seemed certain that the Baron would not survive his heart attack. True, he was much older than his wife, but that didn't mean the worst had to happen.

How awful to be simply written off like that, she thought, shuddering. But at least he didn't know. No one had actually stopped him in the street and told him he was no longer wanted, and that the whole of Paris was discussing his successor.

'Madame?' Marcel was coming towards her, cap in hand, his face a picture of concern. 'Are you ill?'

It was useless to pretend that everything was fine and perfectly normal when you were leaning against a wall, trembling like a leaf, with your face every shade between white and green.

She said, 'I felt giddy for a moment, that's all.'

He was all solicitude, helping her to the car, and keeping a wary eye on her in the mirror as he drove home, ultra-carefully.

Probably doesn't want me being sick over his precious upholstery, Philippa thought, torn between laughter and tears.

He must have used the car telephone while she was on her way up to the apartment, because when she got there Madame Giscard was waiting in obvious agitation.

Before Philippa knew what was happening, she was lying on her bed, with her shoes removed, the curtains drawn, a cloth fragrant with cologne across her

forehead, and a tisane steaming gently on the table
beside her. She had no idea what was in it, but the
herbal infusion was refreshing and oddly relaxing, and
in spite of her inner turmoil she found herself slipping
into a light doze. But dreams pursued her even there,
and she found herself running endlessly down the
shadowy nave of some great cathedral, trying to reach
the altar where Alain stood waiting, but not, as she
realised, when he looked past her, his hand stretched
out in welcome—not for her.

She cried out his name, in anguish, and heard him
answer. Dazedly she opened her eyes, and found him
bending over her.

'What's the matter? Madame Giscard tells me
Marcel found you ill in the street.'

'Not really.' Hastily Philippa struggled into a sitting
position. 'I just felt—odd for a moment. It's nothing.'

'Isn't it?' He sat down on the edge of the bed, his
brows drawing together in a frown. He was silent for
a moment. 'Philippa, tell me—is it possible you could
be—*enceinte*?'

Swift colour rose in her face. 'No—no, of course
not.' For a moment she thought the concern in his
face was for her, then she saw the unguarded relief
that replaced it, and the hope shrivelled.

Of course, she thought, anger building inside her
again, a pregnant wife would be that much more difficult to discard. And if there's to be a baby, he wants
it to be born from the woman he loves—always sup-
posing she's prepared to spoil her figure for nine
months.

She said curtly, 'Fortunately, it's hardly likely.'

'No?' He was still frowning, his mouth twisting
cynically as he looked at her. 'Well, you know best

about that, of course.' He stared down at the floor, for a moment, then said slowly, 'I will leave you to rest now, *ma femme*, but soon—very soon, we must talk seriously, you and I.'

Her heart skipped a beat. She said with a little gasp, 'It really isn't necessary...'

'Ah, but you are wrong,' Alain cut across her, his smile half wintry, half rueful. 'I assure you, *ma chère*, there is all the necessity in the world.' He lifted her hand, kissed it lightly, and left the room.

Left to herself again, Philippa cradled her hand against her cheek, fighting back her tears. She knew what he wished to discuss, and she wanted to tell him that there would be no problem. He could have his divorce, and except for a proviso that Gavin's treatment should continue as long as necessary she wouldn't ask for a thing.

Just my freedom, she thought, as quickly and easily as possible.

Only it wasn't possible, she acknowledged, as she lay staring sightlessly into the gathering darkness of the evening. Because leaving Alain would be like wrenching herself apart, and she knew, in her heart, that she would never be free again.

She was woken the next morning by Madame Giscard with a breakfast tray.

'That's very kind of you,' she said awkwardly, sitting up.

'It is nothing, *madame*.' She received a searching look. 'How are you this morning.'

'Oh, fine. I must have had a slight migraine.'

Madame's usually vinegary face registered an expression of disappointment, fleeting but unmistakable as she left the room.

Good God, Philippa thought as she sipped her chilled apricot juice. They've all been thinking that I'm pregnant!

But, unlike Alain, she thought sadly, Madame Giscard had been hoping it was true. Perhaps that impassive, well-trained exterior concealed a much softer side to her nature.

As she reached for the croissants, Philippa realised that there was an envelope propped beside them, with a note attached in Alain's handwriting.

'This arrived this morning,' it said. 'I think you will agree that it changes a great deal. I shall not return home until late this evening, so perhaps you will be ready to discuss it with me tomorrow.' It was signed simply with his initial.

Like an office memo, Philippa thought wryly, but the fact remained that it was one of the few written communications she had ever received from him, and that made it, in its own way, precious.

As she extracted the typewritten pages from the envelope, she realised with a shock that they formed a detailed report from Gavin's clinic.

A lot of the medical jargon used meant little to her, but the summary at the end was more explicit and comprehensible.

The course of treatment, although experimental, had been largely successful with no damaging side-effects, she read. The amount of drugs being used was now being severely reduced, and replaced with an intensive course of physiotherapy, to which the patient was responding extremely well. The physician in charge of Mr Roscoe's case saw no reason why he should remain at the clinic for any longer than another few weeks, although the patient would continue to require a qualified course of medication, probably for the rest of his life, and it was also desirable that the physiotherapy régime should continue after his return home.

Philippa saw the words 'return home' through a blur of sudden tears. Gavin's well, she thought incredulously. They're sending him home. He can take up his life—paint again.

Breakfast forgotten, she pushed back the bed-clothes and swung her feet to the floor. Zak, she thought. I'll phone him at once. He'll be so thrilled. She grabbed up her robe and sped into the hall. The morning paper was lying beside the telephone, and as she grabbed the receiver it fell to the floor. Impatiently she bent to retrieve it. It had been folded to one of the inside pages, and Henri de Somerville-Resnais' face looked starchily out from the news column.

She knew what that meant immediately. She knelt to the floor and read the brief obituary. It spoke of his service to the government, and his military honours in Indo-China. It mentioned his widow, and the fact that he had died childless. It stated that his estates and personal fortune would now pass to a cousin.

Philippa replaced the paper gently on the table and stared sightlessly at the blank wall. There had been, she thought detachedly, so much it hadn't said. Like the grieving widow's plans to remarry. Was that where Alain had gone—to be with Marie-Laure? Was that why he would not be back until late? If so, it was frankly indecent.

Marie-Laure is free, and Gavin is cured, she thought. That cancels all obligations on both sides. That's what he's going to tell me tomorrow.

She got slowly to her feet. Suddenly she felt bitterly, frighteningly cold, and she tightened the sash of her robe with a shiver.

Well, perhaps she wasn't prepared to stand meekly by and wait to be given her marching orders. Maybe she didn't want to watch Marie-Laure step triumphantly into her shoes. To know that everyone was talking about her, pitying her, laughing at her. Oh, no, that was too much to expect.

She thought, I've got to get out. I can't stand it otherwise.

She wandered into the *salon*. Across the room, her father's painting of the bridge at Montascaux blazed in its sunlit glory. Every time she entered the room her eyes were drawn to it, and she found herself smiling at the memories it evoked.

She thought, I shall miss it, when I go...and paused, with a little gasp, as sudden excitement replaced the chill within her.

She needed somewhere to go. And Zak had told her she needed time on her own to paint. Well, that was what she would do. She would take the bare necessities from her wardrobe, and enough cash from Alain's overly generous allowance to subsist on, and she'd go back to Montascaux. She'd rent somewhere in the locality—the house in the clouds if it was available—and just paint, go for broke, see if she could make it, exactly as her father had done before her.

She swallowed. And perhaps, by the time Gavin was well enough to leave the clinic and come home, she would have a roof to offer him, and a place where they could both work—get back on their feet again.

We'll share a studio, she thought. Just as we always planned.

Perhaps Gavin need never even know about Alain, she thought hopefully. That was a wound she would prefer to remain private.

Not for the first time, she wished she could drive. It would be so much easier to put a travelling bag and her painting things in a car, rather than tote them on a long and probably complicated train journey.

And she would have the painful satisfaction of knowing that it was she who had walked away from the marriage. Alain would not get the chance to dismiss her from his life, because she would be leaving first. And although he would undoubtedly be relieved that she'd taken matters into her own hands, she had little doubt that his pride would be dented just the same.

I'm glad, she thought savagely. I hope everyone laughs at him.

She took one last look at the picture, then turned away. She had to get dressed. She had plans to make.

Zak raised his eyebrows when she told him her decision.

'It's the right idea, honey, but I'm not sure about your motives,' he told her. 'Going away is one thing, running away is another.'

Philippa shrugged insouciantly in reply. 'Desperate situations call for desperate measures,' she countered. 'That's turning into my life's philosophy.'

'Oh, really?' He sent her a sceptical look. 'Well, don't forget your life drawing is also pretty desperate and could use some work. Try and find yourself a model locally.' He swept her into a bear-like hug. 'And come back strong.'

Fabrice was waiting for her at the café. He rose as she approached the table, his face serious.

'Philippa, you have seen the morning paper?'

'Yes, I've seen it.' She sat down and he signalled the waiter to bring their coffee. 'Fabrice, I've something to tell you. I'm going away, very soon, down to the south-west. I'm planning to rent a house there and do some painting.'

He looked totally taken aback. 'You mean—you are leaving your husband?'

She shrugged. 'I'm going away to work. I need to be on my own.'

'No.' Fabrice leaned towards her, his face intense. 'You should not be alone. You are too young, too lovely for that. Philippa—*chérie*—not all men are as uncaring as Alain de Courcy. Let me prove it to you. I want to be with you—to love you.'

Philippa bit her lip, concealing her dismay. She supposed she should have seen this coming.

'No, Fabrice,' she said gently. 'It's quite impossible. I don't need—a relationship.'

'Not yet, perhaps, but there will come a time, and I can be patient.' He reached out and took her hand, stroking the palm gently with his thumb. 'Let me come with you, Philippa. Let me care for you and protect you. I won't make any demands of you, I swear. It will all be exactly as you want. I have some vacation I can take whenever I please. I could drive you to wherever you want to go, as soon as you wish. Tomorrow, if it pleases you.'

She stared at him. The offer was a tempting one, although fraught with difficulties. Fabrice undoubtedly thought that he wouldn't have to be patient for too long, and that it would only be a matter of time before isolation and proximity delivered her into his hand like a ripe plum. Well, he would soon discover his mistake.

And if she seriously wanted to hit back at Alain—damage his pride—what better way than this? There was a kind of poetic justice in letting him think she was leaving him for another man.

'You'd be very bored,' she said slowly. 'I intend to work, very seriously. I'm going to hire a model and...'

'But I could help,' he said eagerly. 'I can cook for us. I could even be your model. Why not?'

Philippa could think of any number of reasons, but she kept them to herself.

There would also be several advantages attached to leaving Paris with Fabrice. If she took a train, Alain would be able to trace her, and she didn't want that. She wanted to vanish from his life at least temporarily, leaving just a note to say that her lawyers would eventually be contacting him about the divorce. She didn't want any recriminations, or any pressure on her to stay and act as camouflage until Marie-Laure could be considered officially out of mourning. Not that he could pressure her any more—not now that Gavin was almost cured. But he could try and persuade her...

A small shiver tingled down her spine. She could not bear that. She needed to get away, and soon. And she could handle Fabrice, couldn't she?

She looked at him across the table, and smiled. 'Tomorrow,' she said, 'would suit me very well. As early as you can make it.'

The die, she thought, was cast.

CHAPTER EIGHT

THE RAIN began just south of Périgueux. Watching it lash relentlessly against the windscreen, Philippa thought it matched her mood almost ideally.

She stole a sidelong look at her companion. He was on edge too, she'd noticed, using the rear-view mirror with almost paranoid intensity. Perhaps he was beginning to think eloping with the wife of Alain de Courcy wasn't the most sensible thing he'd ever done in his life, she thought with wry sympathy. If so, he might not mind too much when she told him, as she would have to, that there was no place for him in her life, even on a temporary basis.

All the way from Paris, she had tried hard to justify her use of Fabrice on the grounds that she might, one day in the far distant future, fall in love with him. But she knew that it would never happen. She belonged to Alain and she always would do, even though he didn't want her.

What a mess it all is! she thought, watching the rain with weary distaste.

But she had to admit that her escape had gone without a hitch. Fabrice had been a tower of strength. While she'd dashed around buying the painting equipment she needed, he had telephoned Madame Béthune in Montascaux to ascertain on Philippa's behalf if the house in the clouds was available for letting. Madame Béthune had remembered Mademoiselle Roscoe with the greatest pleasure, and had assured him the house could be hers for at least two months.

With her painting gear safely stowed in Fabrice's car, all Philippa had to concern herself with was a small travelling bag. She'd packed jeans, shirts, a couple of warm sweaters, some light canvas shoes, and her toilet things. Not one item had come from her trousseau—she'd made sure of that. She'd left her wedding pearls, her engagement ring and every other piece of jewellery Alain had given her, along with a brief note stating baldly that she was going away with another man—well, it was almost the truth, she thought defensively—and asking him not to look for her.

She had, however, retained her wedding ring, slipping it into the purse section of her wallet. It was foolish, she knew, but she needed something to keep— to remember always.

More practically, she had drawn enough money from her account to keep her, with a certain amount of austerity, for the next two months.

After that she would have to become self-sufficient. There was always a market among the tourists who flocked to the south-west of France for original paintings of local views, and she would try to exploit that, she told herself optimistically.

Her departure from the apartment, not long after dawn that morning, had been magically simple, aided by the fact that Alain, once again, had not spent the night at home.

Trying to subdue the pain of that by telling herself she should be grateful, Philippa had dealt noiselessly with locks, bolts and the security system, and sped to where Fabrice was waiting with the car.

She had wondered what she would do if he'd started being amorous on the journey, but she needn't have worried. He had been surprisingly subdued, even *distrait*. He was obviously far more concerned about being followed than playing the lover, and she had to be thankful for that. All the same, she wished his behaviour was rather less agitated.

'Do calm down,' she said, half amused, half irritated as he cast yet another glance rearwards. 'There's no one after us. My guess is that, if Alain's going to bother to look for me, he'll think I'm on my way back to England, and check the Channel ports.'

'How can we tell what he will do?' Fabrice muttered. He sounded sulky and a bit scared, and totally lacking in the boyish charm he had exhibited in Paris. Will the real Fabrice de Thíery please stand up, Philippa thought ruefully.

She had wanted to stop for a meal, but he'd insisted that instead they buy some bread, pâté, and cheese from an *alimentation* and hold a hasty picnic on a roadside verge.

But she couldn't complain about his driving. Maybe it was fear that had kept his foot down on the accelerator, but they had made very good time, and would arrive at Montascaux before it was dark. Madame Béthune had promised to leave a supply of provisions at the house, and if Fabrice could calm his nerves sufficiently, he could demonstrate his prowess as a chef, Philippa thought drily.

She was accustomed to Montascaux bathed in sunshine as her father had painted it. It was odd to find the familiar streets almost deserted under grey skies, and the rain falling harder than ever.

They crossed the bridge and turned the car off the narrow road up the steep and winding track which led to the house.

Philippa's heart lifted excitedly as she leaned forward, waiting for the familiar outline of the building to come into view. It was like coming home, she thought.

It was a simple house, built with the typically steeply sloping tiled roof of the region, and with a *pigeonnier* attached. It was the unconverted upper storey of the *pigeonnier* that Gavin had used as a studio, and she herself would work in.

'Stay here,' Fabrice instructed tersely as he brought the car to a halt in front of the house. 'I will take in the baggage.'

It took two trips, and Philippa sat watching guiltily as Fabrice struggled through the downpour. When he returned he brought an umbrella.

'Use this.' He handed it to her. 'I will put the car in the barn at the back.'

She heard the engine start as she ran headlong for the house. She almost threw herself through the open door into the only living-room. The range had been lit, giving off a cheerful glow, and there was an appetising aroma coming from the stove, where one of Madame Béthune's cassoulets must be cooking slowly.

Philippa gave a little sigh of relief as she glanced round, closing her dripping umbrella. Nothing had really changed, she thought, recognising with pleasure the old-fashioned dresser with its blue and white china, and the big central table covered in oilcloth.

She put the umbrella in the sink, dropped her shoulder-bag on to the table, and started towards the narrow wooden stairs with her travel bag. Two bedrooms and a tiny bathroom had been built into the high-raftered roof space. She opened the door of the larger bedroom and shouldered her way in. The massive bed had been made up in readiness by Madame Béthune, topped by a snowy drift of duvet.

Philippa surveyed it wryly. It really was enormous— far too big for single occupation—and, together with the *armoire*, it took up nearly all the available space.

Shrugging, she put her bag down in the corner and went across the landing to check on the other room. She pushed open the door and paused, her lips tightening. The single bed was stripped to the bare mattress.

And yet she had told Fabrice quite plainly to ask Madame to prepare both rooms. There could, of course, have been a simple breakdown in communication.

On the other hand, Fabrice, in spite of all his chivalrous protestations, could be trying to force some kind of showdown. To undermine her resistance by presenting her with a *fait accompli*. Well, he could just think again!

The drumming of the rain on the roof sounded very loud, suddenly, and very forlorn.

It occurred to her, not for the first time, that she had been stupidly reckless to come to such an isolated spot with a man about whom she knew so little. Her desperate need to escape from Paris, to salvage her pride by taking the initiative, by leaving Alain before he could tell her to go, had clouded her judgement badly.

The last thing in the world she wanted, she realised ruefully, was to spend even one night under the same roof as Fabrice. She was grateful for his help, but that was as far as it went, or ever would go.

She sighed. She would have to offer Fabrice a meal, she supposed, and then she would ask him bluntly to go—to find himself a room for the night in Montascaux, even if she had to dip into her small hoard of money to pay for it.

She hoped, without much conviction, that he'd go quietly, without a scene. She'd promised nothing, of course, but by coming away with him like this she had placed herself in a hopelessly compromising position.

She heard the door downstairs close, and squared her shoulders. She would go down and face him, rather than let him come upstairs and find her, she decided without enthusiasm.

She took a deep breath and descended the stairs, mentally rehearsing what to say. He was standing with his back to her, shaking the water from his raincoat. Now that she was alone with him here, he seemed taller, broader—altogether more formidable in these cramped and homely surroundings, or was that simply a delusion produced by her private fears?

She swallowed. 'Fabrice——' Even in her own ears, her voice sounded thin and strained. 'Fabrice, I've been thinking . . .'

The words broke off in her throat, as he turned without haste to face her. Her hand reached for the banister rail, clutched it until the knuckles turned white. The sound of the rain was extinguished by the terrified throbbing of her pulses, as she stared at him. Not a figment of her imagination, she thought wildly, but there standing in front of her, flesh, blood, bone and sinew. Dear God—*Alain!*

He said softly, unsmilingly, 'You have been thinking, *madame*? Well, I imagine you have plenty of food for thought.'

'You!' Philippa's voice cracked. 'What are you doing here?'

'Where else should a husband be but at his wife's side?' He draped the discarded raincoat over a chair, and took a step towards her.

Philippa recoiled. 'Don't come near me,' she said hoarsely. 'Where is Fabrice?'

Alain shrugged. 'On the first stage of his journey back to Paris, I presume. You find that a matter for regret, perhaps.' His lips twisted mockingly. 'I am sorry, *ma femme*. I shall have to make sure I provide—adequate consolation.'

The words seemed to hang in the air between them. Suddenly the thin wooden rail beneath her fingers seemed the only touch of stability in a reeling world.

She flung her head back. 'I don't need consoling. I want nothing from you, Alain, but my freedom. Our divorce can be as quick and painless as you wish. You've given my father back to me, and I won't ask for anything else, I swear. Just a clean break.'

'How simple you make it sound,' he said softly. 'But perhaps I'm not quite so ready to give you up. You may want nothing more from me, but I want a great deal from you.'

'You must be mad!' The beat of her heart was suddenly unsteady. 'What can I say to convince you that this—farce we've been playing is over? I've left you, Alain. I'm starting a new life. I—I don't know how you found me...'

'Oh, that is quite simple,' he said coolly. 'Ever since that curious attempt at a robbery, I've been having you and your gallant rescuer watched.'

'You've done what?' Her voice rose. 'Oh, I don't believe it!'

'Why not? Did you really think I would take no steps to protect my interests—that I would just relinquish you?' His voice was sardonic. 'It has all been most instructive, believe me, especially my interview late last night with your supposed lover. You really must learn to be less trusting, *ma chérie*. A young man so easily bought is not worthy of you.'

'Bought?' Her lips framed the word incredulously. 'I don't understand.'

'That is obvious,' he said drily. 'I hope you did not care for him too much, Philippa. Not when he was being paid by my uncle to seduce you.'

She cried out, and sank down on the stairs. She said hoarsely, 'You're lying.'

'If I am, then why isn't he here, fighting for you? Telling me to get to hell out of your life?' Alain sounded very tired suddenly. 'No, your account of the robbery aroused my suspicions. It was all—too convenient, too pat. So I had enquiries made, and I discovered that your Fabrice was being employed by Uncle Louis—was visiting him daily, presumably to report on his progress in your affections.'

'I don't believe it!' Philippa beat one fist against another. 'Why should your uncle do such a thing? It makes no sense.'

'To him, it makes a great deal of sense,' Alain said with a shrug. 'He wishes to see our marriage destroyed. It seems he has been telling everyone that my infidelities are making you wretched, that you are near to breaking point. He speaks of you with concern and compassion—the innocent betrayed bride of his womanising nephew. He says that you are desolate, near to breaking point—that you would be totally justified if you left me. Then—*voilà*—you run away, and my uncle has just the scandal he is hoping for. Once again he can attack, leaving my reputation in shreds, holding me up as morally unfit to be in charge of De Courcy International. And those who listened to him last time will listen again, this time, perhaps, with more attention.'

Philippa drew a harsh breath. 'No one—no one could be that devious. I won't believe a word of it.'

'I thought you might say that.' Alain drew an envelope from his inside coat pocket. 'So I took the precaution of having your boyfriend make a sworn statement in writing about his part in the affair. He was completely frank. Do you want to read it?'

Philippa shuddered. 'No.'

'Don't be too disillusioned, *chérie*. He seems to have genuinely enjoyed the pleasure of your company.' He paused. 'I hope you did not make his task too easy for him.' He smiled as he spoke, but the green eyes were emerald-hard.

Philippa bent her head. 'If you were having me watched, and you've read his statement, then you already know the answer to that.'

'Nevertheless, I would like your personal reassurance.' His voice was implacable. 'Tell me, *ma femme*, did you, in fact, give this—Fabrice your body?'

'No,' she said dully.

'Ah, then this would have been your first time together. *Ma pauvre petite*, have I ruined your idyll?'

His tone mocked her. 'In that case, the least I can do, having deprived you of your lover, is to provide a replacement.'

'What do you mean?' Philippa's mouth was suddenly dry.

'I mean that I do not accept that our marriage is over. *Au contraire*, it is about to begin.' Alain gave the room a measuring look. 'This is not, perhaps, the place I would have chosen for our honeymoon, but it will serve.'

'Honeymoon?' Philippa's voice rose in outrage. She got jerkily to her feet. 'What game are you playing now, Alain?'

'No game at all. You are my wife, and while you remain so you will belong to no other man. It is time, I think, that I made that clear to you.'

'And it's time I made something clear as well,' Philippa said furiously. 'I came here to start a new life for myself—to paint—to try and make a home for my father when he comes back from the States. There's no place for you here.'

'Yet there was a place for Fabrice de Thiéry,' he said silkily.

'Not in the way that you think.' She glared at him. 'And who are you to play dog in the manger anyway, after the way you—you...' She stopped, and took a breath. 'I needed a car ride down here, and Fabrice was going to—keep house and model for me. That's all.'

'Ah, no, *ma belle*. You are not that naïve. And nor am I.'

'Think what you like,' she told him defiantly, banishing the memory of her own misgivings to the back of her mind. 'But please don't judge me by your own low standards. I don't want a lover. I came here to work. To re-start my life.'

'And what about our life together?' His voice was quiet.

'We don't have a life.' Philippa bit her lip. 'I'm not your wife, Alain. I never have been. The best thing we can do is let each other go. Then you can be free to marry your—your lady.'

'It's good to know I have your permission,' Alain said slowly. 'But are you so sure she'll want to marry me? After all, she's now a wealthy widow.'

Philippa looked down at the floor, an unwelcome image of Marie-Laure locked in Alain's arms on that moonlit terrace looming uncomfortably large in her mind. 'That's entirely your own business,' she said in a low voice.

'That is true,' he said. 'But you and I also have some business—some unfinished business—to discuss, *ma femme*.'

'I can't think what,' she flung at him. 'I should have thought you'd be glad—grateful that I've taken myself out of your life. You can be happy now— there's nothing and no one to prevent you any longer. And your uncle won't dare make another scandal once you and the Baronne are safely married.'

Alain raised his eyebrows. 'You have it all worked out, it seems.'

'I've had a lot of time to think about it—to consider the best thing to do.'

Alain gestured around him. 'And this is it?'

'I think so.' She lifted her chin. 'It isn't your kind of environment, of course, but then you weren't invited to come here.'

'I need no reminder of that,' Alain said with a touch of grimness. 'May I remind you of the terms of our original agreement?'

Philippa folded her arms defensively across her body. 'I'm not going to go back to Paris and just wait to be divorced,' she said. 'There's nothing to keep us together any more. Gavin is better now, and for that I—I'm grateful, and I always will be. I've done my best to play the part you wanted, and I'm sorry if you don't feel you've had your money's worth in return. Because that's all there is. Frankly, I can't take any more.'

'I was not thinking in terms of value,' he said slowly. 'You seem to have forgotten that when I first proposed marriage to you, I told you that one day I would ask you to give me a child.'

The breath caught in her throat as she stared at him incredulously. 'No—no, I hadn't forgotten, but naturally, under the circumstances, that doesn't apply any more. You can't expect me...'

'Why not?' His voice was gentle, but the green eyes were cool, unwavering.

She tried to laugh. 'Why, because you have a whole new life ahead of you. When you marry again, you can start a family.'

'Perhaps the bride in question has other ideas,' Alain said drily. 'Henri was desperate for an heir all the time they were married, but he died childless in the end.'

So he wasn't blindly besotted after all, Philippa thought with a swift pang of desolation. He knew Marie-Laure for what she was, yet he wanted her just the same. She thrust the thought away.

'That's something you'll need to discuss with her,' she said stiffly. 'It can't concern me.'

'But it concerns you very deeply, *ma chère*.' Alain leaned against the kitchen table, very much at his ease, a faint smile playing about his lips. 'You speak as if our divorce and my remarriage was a certainty—a *fait accompli*. Yet it is nothing of the kind. Perhaps I am content with what I have, and do not wish to change. Have you thought of that?'

She said jerkily, 'But that can't be right. You can't want things to stay as they are—no one could. You must want to be happy—to have a real marriage with the woman you love.'

'Of course,' he agreed. 'But if that is not possible, I would not be the first man to settle for second best.'

'But perhaps I'm not prepared to settle for that.' Philippa gave him a stormy look. 'Maybe I don't want to be the meek little wife, dutifully turning a blind eye to her husband's liaisons. Have *you* thought of that?'

'Meek,' Alain murmured, 'is hardly a word to describe you, *mon amour*.'

'I'm glad you appreciate that,' she said. 'And I'm certainly not going to allow myself to be—used as a—vehicle for childbearing...'

'How mechanical you make it sound!' He had the audacity to laugh out loud.

'Obscene is the word I would use.' Her voice shook. 'How many times must I say it? I've left you, Alain. I should never have agreed to this marriage in the first place. You must see what a terrible mistake it's been.'

'Oh, yes.' He nodded. 'But it is a mistake we must continue to endure for a while.' He paused. 'At least until I have my son.' The green eyes slid slowly, appraisingly down her body and she felt every inch of skin warm under his glance. 'Would it really be such a hardship to give him life?'

Anguish wrenched at her as she contemplated what he was asking. In different circumstances it would be paradise, the summation of all her secret, wildest dreams. But in reality, knowing that he didn't love her—that she was just the convenient wife he was using—it would be sheer unmitigated hell.

She looked back at him and shrugged. 'I've made my plans for the future,' she said. 'And nothing you can say or do is going to change my mind, Alain. It's over.'

'You speak with great certainty,' he said. 'Yet, *mignonne*, for the first time in this strange marriage of ours we are together and completely alone. As the days pass—and the nights—don't you think it is possible I might—persuade you to be a little kinder to me?'

'What kindness has there ever been between us?' Sudden bitterness vibrated in her voice, and she saw him wince.

'Very little, it is true, but it does not always have to be like this. We could—try again.'

There was an odd note in his voice—wistful, almost humble, and Philippa caught her breath. At that moment all she wanted to do was cross the floor space which separated them, and go into his arms. It would be the simplest action in the world—and also the most fatal. Snatching at her control, she went on the attack.

'And what about Madame de Somerville-Resnais? Have you got her permission for this touching reconciliation?'

'Hardly,' Alain returned curtly. 'She is in seclusion.'

'Oh, I see.' Philippa got to her feet. Her moment of weakness, of yearning, was over, and she was angry again. 'How stupid of me! You can't really continue your affair while she's in mourning, so you thought you'd entertain yourself with me. What a novel twist! It isn't usually the wife who's the little bit on the side.'

'How dare you!' Alain took a step towards her, his face darkening. 'Listen to me, you little fool...'

'I've heard enough. I want you to go, Alain. Go— now. Don't you understand?'

'It's you who doesn't understand. In the name of God, Philippa I've come all this way to see you—to talk to you...'

'Then you've had a wasted journey.' He took another step towards her, and she recoiled violently, backing away up the stairs, her hands flung rigidly out in front of her as if pushing him away. 'No!' Her voice rose hysterically. 'Don't touch me—don't come near me...'

The words died into a deep silence. Alain halted, staring at her, his brows drawn into a frown of utter incredulity, horror dawning in his eyes.

'Mon Dieu,' he whispered at last. 'You're afraid of me. Do you truly find me so terrifying—so repulsive?'

She shivered. 'Just go—please.' Her voice broke.

'Very well.' His voice was quiet. 'If that is what you wish.' He picked up his damp raincoat and shrugged it on, his eyes never leaving her. Then he walked to the door.

At the doorway he turned. His lips were smiling, but his face was as bleak as winter.

'It's ironic, isn't it,' he said. 'Of all the women in the world, my wife is the one I cannot reach. Goodbye, ma belle, and good luck.'

Philippa watched the door close behind him. When she was alone, she came downstairs, feeling her way across the room to a chair as if she was blind.

Alain had gone. She had been strong enough— brave enough to send him away. And now all she had to face was the lonely consequences of that courage— every day that remained of her life.

CHAPTER NINE

SHE was still sitting, gazing into space, when the door was flung roughly open again a few minutes later and Alain strode in, his face like thunder.

Shocked, Philippa jumped to her feet, knocking the chair over backwards with a clatter.

He faced her grimly across the table, eyes blazing, lifting a hand to silence her as her lips parted to speak.

'Yes, I've come back, but not of my own will, I assure you, so kindly spare me the recriminations that I'm certain are forming on that vitriolic little tongue of yours.'

'It—it isn't that.' Her voice quivered. 'But you can't blame me for being surprised. I thought you were returning to Paris.'

'So did I. But it seems your would-be lover has other ideas.' He paused. 'All four tyres on my car have been slashed. I shall be going nowhere tonight.'

'Fabrice did that?' Philippa bit her lip. 'But why?'

He shrugged curtly. 'Spite, I imagine. A futile act of revenge because I'd found him out—spoiled his little game with you.' He gave her an icy smile. 'Perhaps I've misjudged him, *ma femme*. Perhaps it wasn't simply the money my uncle was paying him. Maybe he really wanted you for himself.'

'I hope you don't expect me to feel flattered,' Philippa flung back at him. 'I'm sorry about your car, but it isn't the end of the world. There's a garage in Montascaux. They'll supply you with more tyres.'

'I'm sure they will,' he said. 'Tomorrow.'

He let the word sink in, nodding sardonically at the transparent look of dismay on her face. 'No, *chérie*, I do not propose to walk in this rain all the way to the village to a garage that will undoubtedly be shut by now.'

'It may not be . . .' she began.

'But I am not prepared to prove it, one way or the other, tonight,' Alain said silkily. 'Much as we may both regret the necessity, I am about to become your overnight guest.'

'Oh, but you can't!' Her hands twisted together in distress. 'Surely you could spend the night in your car—or there's an *auberge* further up the valley.'

'I hope its business flourishes,' said Alain, too courteously. 'It will not, however, be receiving my custom. Nor will I be risking cramp and pneumonia in the car. You are not very hospitable, *ma chère*.'

She flushed. 'You can hardly expect it.'

'And neither,' Alain went on with a trace of acid, 'can you expect me to force my attentions on a girl who has spent the last half-hour cowering from me. I had enough of that on our wedding night, if you remember. And since.' He paused deliberately, his brows lifting sardonically as she flinched. 'So please stop looking at me as if you were a mouse, and I were a hungry cat, and let us try and behave like civilised human beings for what remains of the evening.'

'You could have slashed your own tyres,' Philippa said mutinously.

He sighed. 'Yes, and I could also have arranged the rain, and the lateness of the hour, all for the pleasure of a few more enforced hours in your company, my little shrew. However, I did none of these things.' He walked round the table and picked up the fallen chair. 'So please be less nervous.' He nodded towards the stove. 'Are we going to eat that food, or let it burn?'

Philippa shrugged defeatedly. 'I suppose we're going to have supper.'

'Well, we have eaten together many times before. It won't be such an ordeal,' he said drily. 'The difference is there'll be no Henriette to wait on us.'

'No,' she said. She was remembering what he'd said—that for the first time in their marriage they were together and completely alone, and the prospect terrified her.

He thinks I'm afraid of him, she thought. But he's so wrong. I'm frightened of myself—scared of betraying everything I feel for him. Because if he knew, then I'd be in his power forever, and I couldn't endure that. I'm not going to be a complaisant wife pretending that every time he doesn't come home, he's working late at the office. I'd rather live apart from him than put up with that kind of lie.

She found place mats and cutlery, and laid the table. Alain cut up the baguette which Madame Béthune had supplied in the box of provisions, and opened a bottle of red wine.

The sheer easy domesticity of it caught her by the throat. She found herself thinking, If only... and thrust the thought away before it could become concrete in her mind. This was what she'd dreaded, she thought. The ordinary intimacy of preparing for a meal together. This was what real marriages were about. This was danger.

The cassoulet was thick and rich with preserved goose, just as Philippa remembered. In spite of her inner turmoil, she ate well. Apart from a few appre-

ciative comments about the food, Alain made no
attempt to engage her in conversation, and she was
grateful for that. They finished the meal with cheese
and fruit and the rest of the bread.

'Coffee?' Alain pushed back his chair and reached
for the jug and filter unit.

'Do you know how to make it?' Philippa couldn't
keep the astonishment out of her voice.

'Of course,' he said with asperity. 'It may also surprise you to know, *ma femme*, that I can cook. When
I was a boy I used to go on hunting trips with my
father. He believed in being self-sufficient.'

'Goodness,' she said. 'Did your mother go along
as well?'

He laughed. 'Oh, no. She was like you, *chérie*. She
was interested in painting—in watercolours. It was just
a pastime with her, and I suspect her work had more
charm than talent, but my father thought it was wonderful. He had a whole collection of her work framed
and hung in our house at Fontainebleau.'

She nearly said, 'I wish I could seem them,' and
stopped herself just in time.

She'd wondered about the Fontainebleau estate, and
Alain's other homes too. He'd never suggested they
should visit any of them, she thought, which helped
emphasise how very much on the margin of his life
she lived.

Instead, she said neutrally, 'Did your parents live
at Fontainebleau?'

He nodded. 'All their lives together. It was always
our family home.' There was a nostalgic, almost tender
note in his voice as if he was recalling good memories,
she thought with a slight pang.

Philippa said stiltedly, 'It sounds as if they were very happy together.'

'Yes, I think they were, in spite of everything.' He encountered her questioning look, and shrugged. 'Theirs was an arranged marriage too. In the early days they had problems, but then who does not?' he added with irony.

'Yes,' she said, and pushed back her own chair. 'I—I don't think I'll bother with coffee. It might keep me awake, and I have to start work tomorrow.'

'Such industry,' Alain said softly. 'But you've forgotten one thing. You've still to show me where I'm to sleep.'

'Oh—yes.' She bit her lip. 'There are two rooms, but I'm afraid only one of them has been prepared. Madame Béthune brings the sheets and things from the farm, you see and . . .'

'Only one room.' Alain's lips twisted. '*Le pauvre* Fabrice! I can understand his disappointment, his desire for revenge on me.'

'Well, he was making a big mistake, and so are you,' Philippa said shortly. 'I never had the slightest intention of sleeping with him.'

'I think in this isolated spot, *ma chère*, it might have been wiser to examine Fabrice's intentions.' Alain's voice bit. 'Didn't it occur to you that you might be getting into a situation you couldn't handle?'

She flushed defensively. 'But I'd made the position clear to him. And he'd always seemed so—decent,' she added lamely.

'A paid seducer who slashes tyres.' Alain's smile was grim. 'You wouldn't have had a prayer, you little fool.'

She lifted her chin. 'I was desperate,' she said. 'And when I get desperate I tend to do foolish things—as you should know.'

'Our marriage being an example of prime idiocy on the part of us both.' The sudden bitterness in his voice shocked her. 'Well, show me this room, *madame*. There's a rug in the car. I can manage for one night.'

She nodded silently and led the way upstairs. The door of her own room was standing open, and she saw Alain's glance flick sideways, absorbing the big snowy bed, but he made no comment.

She found herself wondering suddenly, crazily, how she would act, what she would do if Alain took her into his arms, drew her into that room, down on to the yielding softness of that bed...

She said with a little gasp, as she threw open the door of the smaller room, 'Well, this is where you'll sleep, and the bathroom is at the end of the passage. I—I hope you'll be comfortable.'

'That,' he said cuttingly, 'is hardly likely. *Bonsoir*, Philippa.'

She muttered her own hasty goodnight and fled into her room. She was tempted to turn the key in the lock, but it was clearly rusty, and, anyway, she didn't want to overreact.

She heard Alain go downstairs, and return a short while later, presumably with his overnight things and the rug. She heard his footsteps descend the stairs again, and then everything went quiet. She undressed hurriedly, used the bathroom, and crept under the duvet.

But sleep eluded her. It was not going to be easy, she thought, staring into the darkness, to go on pretending that she didn't care—that their marriage was a mistake she was eager to put behind her. Yet somehow it had to be done.

Because the last thing she wanted was to give herself away somehow, and let Alain see that she loved him.

A clean break, she thought. That was what she needed. Something that would heal—eventually.

Only a few more hours, she thought. Only a few more. She kept repeating the words in her head over and over again like some private litany of pain, until at last she fell asleep.

The sun was filtering through the curtains when she opened her eyes the next morning. She glanced at her watch and sat up with a start. It was nearly ten o'clock.

She flung on her clothes and headed for the stairs, pausing to glance into Alain's room. There was no sign of him. Perhaps he'd already left, she thought, her step faltering slightly.

The room downstairs was empty too, but there was a lingering fragrance of coffee in the air, and a bowl and plate washed neatly by the sink, so presumably he'd breakfasted.

She was just making her own coffee when she heard the roar of an engine. Peering through the window above the sink, she saw a large breakdown vehicle edging its way out of the yard, with Alain's car on the back of it.

And a moment later Alain himself came into view, walking slowly, his head bent.

'What's happened?' Philippa swung round to confront him as he came through the door. 'Why have they taken your car away? Haven't they got any tyres for that model?'

'Plenty,' he said. 'That isn't the problem. Your friend Fabrice has also tampered with the engine in some way. They think it will need a new part, and that could take a day or two.'

'Oh, no!' Philippa beat her fist on the draining board in frustration. 'This can't be happening!'

'I assure you it is,' Alain said acidly. 'You are not the only one to be inconvenienced, believe me.'

'But you don't have to wait for the repair. You could hire a car...'

'The car I am driving is valuable to me,' he said curtly. 'I prefer to remain on the spot, where I can keep an eye on what they are doing to it.'

'But you said you'd go. You can't stay here!' She heard the panic in her voice, and tried to laugh. 'I mean—I need to be on my own to work. I told you that.'

'Yet total solitude wasn't your original plan.' Alain's face was cold. 'Do you think you'd have dismissed Fabrice de Thiéry so easily?'

'Perhaps not,' she admitted, with a grimace. 'But he could have been useful.' She saw the derisive look he flung her, and flushed angrily. 'No, not in that way. But he was going to model for me...'

'Model?' His tone was steely. 'When you say that, *ma chère*, do you mean clothed or unclothed?'

Philippa's lips tightened, 'Well, both, actually, but...'

'*Formidable,*' Alain said softly. 'This story gets better and better.'

'It is not a story,' she said between her teeth. 'I need to work on my life drawing—Zak's orders—and for that I need a model. Whom I shall now have to pay.' She gave him a burning look. 'There's nothing salacious about modelling, you know. To a painter the human body is a composition of light and shade—planes and angles.'

'I wonder if that is how de Thiéry would have regarded it,' Alain said coolly. 'Perhaps he might have agreed with me that a naked girl, certainly, should be enjoyed with all the senses, not just the eye.'

'I'm sure that's exactly what you would think,' Philippa retorted with a bite. 'But there weren't going to be any naked girls, and anyway, you're not an artist.'

He laughed. 'I think with my father, *ma belle*, that one artist in the family is enough. Now I shall take my philistine self to the farm in search of proper bedding. I do not intend to spend another night under one small car rug.'

As she poured out her coffee, Philippa watched him cross the courtyard to the gate, moving with that lithe muscled grace she had come to know so well. She sighed. He was beautiful, she thought sadly. That was the only word for it.

Oh, why couldn't he have just accepted her departure from his life and stayed in Paris where he belonged? Why had he followed her here, tormenting her, distracting her—insulting her with his offer that they should continue their soulless arrangement? she asked herself stormily. Every day she was forced to remain under the same roof with him was like a fresh wound.

Work, it seemed, was the only answer.

When she had finished breakfast, she went up into the *pigeonnier*. The house was regularly rented by artists, who used it as a studio, so the big room was neatly swept out.

Philippa hunted round until she found a small table, which she covered with a cream cloth, before beginning to assemble the elements of a still life subject on it. She carried up from the kitchen an earthenware jug, some tumblers, a wine bottle, and a small wicker basket filled with fruit and vegetables. It took some time to arrange these to her satisfaction.

She was standing back, surveying the composition critically, when Alain came up the wooden stairs.

'Madame Béthune was reluctant to issue any more bedding,' he said with faint amusement. 'She was astounded to hear that more than one bed would be used. She's clearly a romantic soul, even if she did insist on addressing me as Monsieur de Thiéry.'

Philippa flushed. 'Yes—well, Fabrice did telephone her originally, so I suppose she thinks...'

'It is quite obvious what she thinks,' Alain drawled. 'She was after all instructed to prepare just one room.'

Philippa's colour deepened. 'Not by me,' she said stonily. 'But fortunately, it's no longer an issue.'

She determinedly switched her attention back to the table. She regarded the arrangement for a moment, then shook her head. 'Something's still not quite right.'

Alain came to stand beside her. 'It lacks height,' he said, after a moment. 'Why not use the bottle as a candlestick?'

'Why, yes,' she said grudgingly, annoyed that he should have noticed something so obvious, when she had overlooked it. Her concentration was shot to pieces, she thought. 'There should be some candles in the kitchen.'

She descended the stairs, tensely aware that he was following, and went through the communicating door into the main part of the house.

There was a limp package lying on the kitchen table. Alain nodded towards it. 'In the guise of Fabrice, I accepted a rabbit for our dinner tonight.'

'Heavens!' Philippa tried to speak lightly as she took some candles from a dresser drawer. 'I've no idea what to do with a rabbit.'

'Ah, but I have,' Alain told her. 'Would you prefer it sautéd with garlic and herbs, or casseroled with a mustard sauce?'

Philippa gulped. 'Er—sautéd, I think,' she said rather faintly.

'Fine,' he said briskly. 'I'll call you when it's ready.'

'You really don't have to bother——' she began, but he interrupted.

'It's my pleasure, *chérie.*' His smile was tinged with irony. 'A little compensation perhaps for making you suffer the inconvenience of my presence.'

Oh, God, she thought. If he only knew... Aloud, she said lamely, 'Well, thank you,' and fled back to the *pigeonnier*.

She made numerous sketches of her subject, from every angle, concentrating hard, but as the afternoon wore on she found she was content with nothing she'd done. The thing looked stilted—random, she thought restively. But at least she'd made a start.

There was the most deliciously savoury smell of cooking drifting through from the kitchen, and she wrinkled her nose in appreciation as she went in.

Alain was seated at the table, slicing carrots into sticks. He glanced round at her. 'Have you finished for the day?' he asked.

'I think so.' She dropped wearily on to the chair opposite and watched him. 'Have you been cooking all afternoon?'

'By no means. I walked down to the village to the *tabac*, then I had a game of boules with some of the local people.'

Philippa stared at him. 'Weren't you bored?' She saw his brows lift, and hurried on, 'I mean, it's so different from the life you're used to. You must feel so—so cut off from your work—from everything.'

'You don't think I'm capable of relaxation?'

'Not exactly,' she said slowly. 'But you always seem so dynamic—so high-powered. I'd have thought you'd find the pace of life round here—frustrating.'

His mouth twisted in amusement. 'If I'm frustrated, *ma belle*, it has nothing to do with the pace of life, believe me.'

To which, Philippa realised with vexation as her face warmed, there was little she could say in reply.

The rabbit was delicious, moist and flavoursome, accompanied by small potatoes cooked in their skins, and the carrots, lightly tossed in butter.

'Some cheese to follow?' Alain watched approvingly, as she mopped up the juices from her plate with a piece of bread.

She shook her head. 'I couldn't manage another thing. You—you really are a good cook.' She hesitated. 'You're a very surprising person sometimes, Alain.'

'Do you think so, *ma chère*?' His tone was dry. 'I got the impression that you found me all too predictable.'

'Oh, no.' She bit her lip. 'I didn't foresee, for one thing, that you'd follow me here.'

'You thought I'd be content simply to abandon you to the dubious attentions of Monsieur de Thíery?' he asked. 'No, Philippa, I told you, if you remember, that we had to have a serious talk, you and I.'

'Yes, but surely that could be conducted through our lawyers.' Her throat felt constricted.

There was a silence, then he said courteously. 'Of course—if that is what you prefer.'

'I—I think so. We have to be realistic, after all.'

'Yes.' He rose and began to clear the table.

'Let me do that.' Philippa got to her feet. 'It's only fair, after all.'

'And you have a strong sense of justice, don't you, *ma femme*? You believe in adhering strictly to the letter of the law in all circumstances. You allow no room for negotiation.' His face was grim as he looked at her.

'I don't understand what you mean.' Her voice faltered slightly.

Alain shrugged. 'It doesn't matter.' He paused. 'If you don't need my help, I think I'll go back to the *tabac* again for a while. There's usually a card game there in the evenings, and it will relieve you of my company for an hour or two.'

She said stiltedly, 'Thank you. I—I suppose you haven't any idea when your car will be ready?'

His face hardened. 'Not yet. It could be a long job, it seems.'

'Oh, God,' she said in a stifled voice, her hands clenching at her side. 'I wish they'd hurry—get it finished...'

He threw back his head and looked at her, his face icily bleak. He said, 'And so do I, *madame*. As God is my witness, so do I. Then, perhaps we will both have some peace.'

The rawness in his voice cut Philippa like a blade. His name formed, achingly, on her lips, but before she could speak it, the door had slammed and he had gone.

CHAPTER TEN

PHILIPPA slept badly that night, tossing and turning, listening restively for Alain's return. She couldn't put out of her mind the frozen starkness of his face as he'd left her.

Nor could she forget how sorely she'd been tempted to run after him—to call him back.

But what would that have achieved, she asked herself, savagely punching her pillow, except more heartbreak in the end?

It was in the small hours when he eventually returned. She heard the door close downstairs, then the sound of his footsteps quietly mounting the wooden stairs.

She lay very still, staring across the room in the darkness, waiting tensely, a wave of mingled terror and half-ashamed excitement invading her body as he paused outside her door.

And if it opened, if he came to her, what would she say? What would she do?

For a long screaming moment the questions beat at her mind, and she could not find an answer. Then, at last, she heard him move away, and his own door open and close, and slowly she released her pent-up breath, and allowed her body to relax from its taut coil.

She had escaped again, it seemed, but not from him. It was from herself, she acknowledged wincingly, as she turned on to her stomach and buried her burning face in the pillow.

Dear God, she thought, I'm going to have to be so careful...

She slept fitfully, and woke early. She dressed and went quietly downstairs, carrying her sandals, so as not to wake Alain. She made herself some black coffee, and then went straight to the studio.

The previous day's work seemed just as unpromising as she'd remembered. She rearranged the table yet again, then fetched a chair and a knife from the kitchen.

She wanted the whole thing to look less static—to appear as if someone had been working at the table, preparing vegetables, but had pushed back the chair and got up for some reason.

She stepped back, nodding, then set up her easel and prepared her palette. She began to work frantically, almost throwing the paint on to the canvas, trying to rid herself of the tensions and uncertainties inside her.

This was the life she had chosen, after all, and she had to make the best of it. She was turning her back on the role of Madame de Courcy, which she had filled so awkwardly, and unsuccessfully, and she had to learn to paint well enough to earn her own living, which was only what she'd always intended. Only Gavin's illness had intervened, with all its disastrous consequences.

Philippa sighed soundlessly. One day, she might even be able to put it all behind her—forget there had ever been a time when she had been Alain's wife. Their strange marriage had only lasted a few months, after all. It wasn't a lifetime she had to recover from.

And she'd taken the first steps on the road to recovery, when she'd left him.

He shouldn't have followed her, talking of honeymoons—babies. It was cynical—despicable, when he knew—none better—that they would never share a real marriage. When he didn't love her.

She found herself wondering what it would have been like if she and Alain had just met—if she'd been here painting, and his car had broken down, and they'd been thrown together somehow.

She halted that train of thought abruptly. If they'd been strangers in passing, Alain would have walked by without a second glance. She was the last woman in the world he would have chosen as his wife. She might have acquired a surface gloss, but underneath she was still the same colourless little nonentity he'd registered with such shock at their first meeting in Lowden Square. Not just plain either, she admitted wretchedly, but sexually frigid as well.

'*Qu'est-ce que tu as?* Are you all right?'

She was so startled at Alain's unheralded arrival in the studio that she almost yelped.

'Do you have to creep up on me like that?' she demanded crossly.

'I made a normal entrance,' he said levelly. 'But you were thinking so deeply that you were oblivious to everything else.'

'Oh.' Her face warmed slightly, and she was thankful he could have no idea of the tenor of her thoughts.

'I've brought you some soup.' He put the tray he was holding down on the table. 'You had no breakfast, and you cannot work without eating.'

'I'm not working very much at all at the moment.' Philippa's nose twitched involuntarily as the rich aroma of the vegetable broth reached her.

'Isn't it going well?' Alain came to stand beside her, surveying the canvas with raised brows.

'As a class exercise it would pass—just,' she said. Or as therapy, she added silently. 'But there's nothing of me—none of the things I want to express in it. As usual, it's—lacking.'

'I think you are too hard on yourself,' Alain said, after a pause. 'Eat your soup, and you'll feel better. Hunger makes one depressed.'

He walked back to the table and picked up the knife. 'So this is where it went. I've been searching for it.'

She said, 'I'm sorry.' Then, as she focused on him properly, she said with a heart-thudding stab of excitement, 'Alain, would you stay there for a moment—like that?'

He glanced round, brows raised. *'Pourquoi?'* he began, then started to laugh as he saw her reach for her sketching block. 'Ah, no, you can't be serious.'

'Never more so.' Her voice was urgent. 'Just stand there—and don't move, please.'

She knew now why the picture wasn't working. Because Alain was missing from it. Because she'd tried to exclude him from it physically—tried to suggest, instead, his personality and vitality without his actual presence.

As soon as she had seen him standing by the table, that had dawned on her with the utmost clarity.

But then, she realised, from the moment she'd seen him in Lowden Square, she had wanted to paint him. It was one of the first things that had occurred to her. And this might be her one and only chance to do it.

She covered sheet after sheet of her block with sketches, gulping down the cooling soup in between at his insistence, making him adopt new positions, sometimes on his feet, sometimes sitting. He was clearly amused, and certainly puzzled, but he complied anyway.

'I demand to be allowed to buy this masterpiece when it is finished,' he said, as he sliced with wry obedience into a tomato. 'I refuse to allow my colleagues and employees at De Courcy to see me publicly in this domestic role.'

'Don't fuss—and turn your head, just a fraction. That's perfect. Now, hold it.'

He sighed. 'Anything you say, *mon amour*. You're quite crazy, do you know that?'

Perhaps I am, Philippa thought unsteadily, but suddenly I'm alive too, and this is going to work. I know it is.

All the time, even in Paris, Alain had been in her head, coming between her and the image she was trying to create in paint. She'd tried to resist him, to banish him from her imagination. But now she knew that she had to paint him, to make him the focal point of this painting at least.

And maybe in this way, she could exorcise him forever.

She worked with a kind of desperation, blocking in the new composition, with Alain seated, his dark face intent on his mundane task, as she had seen him only the night before.

Time went by, and she didn't notice its passage until he said, at last, '*Ma chère*, quite apart from this cramp, which I'm trying to endure for the sake of art, unless I move soon, we will have no dinner.'

'I wasn't thinking,' she admitted ruefully. 'You should have regular breaks. I'm sorry.'

'Oh, don't apologise. I'm sure that suffering is good for me.' He rose to his feet, stretching, and Philippa sank her teeth into her lower lip as she watched the effortless grace of the movement.

She said, faltering a little, 'Would you sit for me again tomorrow—please?'

He gave her a frankly questioning look, then shrugged. 'If that is what you wish.'

Oh, it is, she thought. It is. It may be madness, but it's what I want more than anything else in the world.

She stood, staring at the easel, after he had gone downstairs. It was too early to say whether the painting would be good or bad, but it would be something for her to keep out of the wreck of their marriage. Something to remember him by.

Her stomach constricted painfully. Something to torment herself with through an eternity of loneliness, as well, she thought stonily, and began to clean her brushes.

There was beef in red wine for dinner that night. They conversed politely, like strangers, over the meal. Afterwards, Philippa cleared the table and washed up.

When she turned back to the table, Alain had poured himself some more wine, and was frowning over a chessboard he had unearthed from somewhere.

He said, 'Will you join me?'

'For the wine or the chess?'

He shrugged. 'Either—or both.'

Philippa drew a chair up to the table, accepting the glass of wine he offered her.

'I didn't know you played chess,' she began, then stopped abruptly. It seemed that everything she said to him was designed to draw attention to their total estrangement, and yet that wasn't what she intended at all.

'I enjoy solving the problems the game poses,' he said, after a pause. 'Unlike those of ordinary life, they have an order—a pattern.'

'Yes, I suppose so,' she said stiltedly. 'I used to play a great deal with Gavin.'

He slanted a smile at her. 'I hope he taught you well.'

'Well enough,' Philippa returned, a shade tartly. 'I think I can give most people a run for their money. You may not be as good as you think.'

'Fighting talk!' Alain sounded amused. 'Shall we, then, make the game more competitive by introducing a small bet?'

Philippa frowned. 'What kind of bet?' she asked suspiciously. She touched one of the fists he extended to her, and found to her annoyance that she had chosen black.

'Nothing too extreme,' he said lightly. 'If I lose,' he paused, 'I'll continue to prepare the meals while I remain here.'

She eyed him. 'And if you win?'

'One kiss—freely given.' His hand hovered over the board, waiting to make the first move. The green eyes glittered a challenge. 'Is it a deal? Or haven't you enough confidence in your game?'

'I have every confidence in myself.' Philippa lifted her chin. 'I think you're going to be very tired of cooking before you return to Paris.'

Alain shrugged. 'We'll see.' He moved his king's pawn up to the fourth row, and Philippa did the same. 'Tell me, do you plan to bring your father here when he is finally discharged from the clinic?'

'Yes, I think so. We were always very happy here.'

'And you think you can recapture those past times?' His attention was fixed on the board. He moved his queen to the bishop's position in the third row.

'Why not?' Philippa moved her own queen's pawn to the third row.

Alain shrugged again. 'Because I do not think it's possible to turn back the clock,' he said flatly. 'If it was, then I would too.'

'Resuming your life as a bachelor, no doubt,' Philippa said with something of a snap.

'Exactly.' Alain placed his king's bishop in front of the queen's bishop in the fourth row.

She had not expected him to agree so readily, and stiffened indignantly, her hand hovering over her queen's knight.

'Well, you'll soon be free again,' she said coolly. 'Or would you have preferred never to have been married to me at all?'

'I would have much preferred it, *ma chère*.' His tone was almost casual. 'It was hardly a marriage, after all.'

Philippa sat up very straight. 'Then why did you come chasing after me?' she demanded, moving the knight into the fourth row.

'Because, however unacceptable it had become, we still had a bargain,' he said quietly.

'I kept my side of it.'

'You really think so?' He sounded politely amazed.

'It was you—your fault. You spoiled everything by breaking your word.' That sounded like a childish whinge, she realised with vexation.

'Ah, yes,' he said mockingly. 'I was a brute to you, wasn't I, *chérie*—making you sleep in the same bed with me, forcing you to do those disgusting things. But I was fool enough to think, you see, that maybe we could make our marriage more than some—clause in a contract. You'd have preferred me to obtain your signature in triplicate, perhaps, before I touched you.'

Philippa drew a shaky breath. 'I would have preferred you not to touch me at all.'

'As you made plain each time I ventured to do so,' said Alain, too courteously.

'I hope you don't expect me to apologise for disappointing you?' she flared.

He shrugged. 'Perhaps we should concede that we disappointed each other.'

'That's a concession indeed.' Philippa bit her lip. 'Aren't you afraid of denting your image as the great lover?' She gave a strident little laugh. 'No, of course not—how stupid of me! You have the Baronne to bolster your ego in that direction, of course.'

'Ah,' Alain said softly, 'my beautiful Marie-Laure. Shall I tell you about her, *ma chère*? Every last detail?'

Her face flamed. 'No,' she said, between her teeth. 'That's quite unnecessary, thank you.'

'You seem so obsessed by her that I thought you might find it interesting.' He gave her a level look, then glanced down at the chessboard, his brows raised. 'After all, you've been totally frank with me about your Fabrice, haven't you?'

'That's quite different, and you know it.'

'Do I?' The green eyes glittered at her.

'Yes.' Philippa pushed her chair back, and rose. 'I don't want to hear about Marie-Laure or any of your women, Alain. Can't you understand that?'

'Oh, yes. But there are also some things that you need to understand about me, Philippa.'

'I know all that I need to know,' she said angrily. 'I was just like one of those pawns, wasn't I?' She gestured angrily at the board. 'Something you could use in your chess game against your uncle, and then discard when it was convenient. Only a pawn isn't supposed to say "check" to the king, is it? Which is just what I did when I left you. And that's what you can't forgive. That's why you're here, tormenting me like this. Well, the game's over now, and so is our marriage. And there's nothing you can do about it,' she added recklessly.

'Isn't there?' His smile was silky. 'Well, there is still something left to be won, *mignonne*. And I like to win. So...' he picked up his queen. He said softly, 'White queen to black knight two, *mon amour*. And— checkmate.'

Philippa drew a sharp breath, her attention totally diverted back to the board in front of them. 'But that's not right,' she began. 'You can't have...'

'Fool's mate, *chérie*. I'm sure you've heard of it.'

Oh, yes, she'd heard of it. Avoiding this commonest of traps for the inexperienced was one of the first things Gavin had taught her. And she'd walked straight into it.

'Oh, no!' she wailed. 'Oh, I don't believe it!'

But the board was there in front of her, mute evidence of Alain's swift and humiliating victory.

'Chess requires concentration, *ma belle*. Do you want your revenge on me? Shall we play another game—for another bet, of course.'

'No thanks,' she said curtly. 'One defeat like that is more than enough.' She glanced at her watch. 'Anyway, I'm rather tired. I think I'll go to my room.'

'In a moment,' Alain said gently. 'After I've collected my winnings.'

Philippa bit her lip. In retrospect, it had been foolhardy to agree to any kind of wager, but she'd been so sure she could win, or at least take him to stalemate, that it hadn't seemed really risky. But now...

She swallowed. 'We didn't exactly establish the circumstances,' she began awkwardly. 'I'd be prepared to—kiss you goodbye when you leave.'

'I'm overwhelmed,' he said sardonically. 'But I think a debt of honour should be settled as soon as possible, don't you?'

He pushed his chair back, and got to his feet.

Philippa rose too. She said shakily, 'Alain, wait! I—I didn't think you meant it.'

'How very unwise of you, *ma belle*.' He came to her side, and his hands descended on her shoulders. Her whole body stiffened in resistance, and this reaction was not lost on him.

He said quietly, 'And to fight me, Philippa, would be even more unwise. It's only a kiss, after all.'

His face seemed to swim in front of her suddenly, and she closed her eyes. Only a kiss, she repeated silently. Only a kiss. But, dear God, when was the last time she'd known the painful pleasure of his mouth on hers? It had been such a long time—such an eternity...

His lips were cool and very gentle. They caressed hers with a featherlight touch that enticed and promised.

It isn't fair. The words formed and dissolved in her mind. She would have preferred insistence—even a certain amount of force, something she could resent. Not this—silken seduction. Fool's mate, she thought dizzily, and she was the greatest fool of all.

His hands slid from her shoulders down to her waist, drawing her closer. The kiss deepened, and as her lips parted helplessly under the beguiling pressure, she felt the first sweet, erotic stab of his tongue against hers.

Excitement stirred, catching the breath in her throat. She tried to say 'No,' but all that emerged was a little strained sigh.

Alain lifted a hand, twisting it into her hair, letting the soft strands twine round his fingers. He pulled her head back, making her lie across his arm, supporting her at the waist. He kissed her again, slowly and hotly this time, then let his lips travel down over the long, exposed line of her throat to the opening of her shirt. As his mouth brushed burningly over her vulnerable skin, a shiver of pure weakness trembled through her body.

His teeth tugged at the flimsy shirt buttons, freeing them with almost negligent ease, baring her to the waist.

His mouth closed on her pointed breast, and she cried out sharply. The tug of his lips on her flesh, the stroke of his tongue across her hardening nipple, was a fierce and painful delight. She wanted it to stop. She wanted it to go on forever.

She found herself remembering, with total, shaming recall, just how Alain's body felt, sheathed inside her own.

His hand moved down her body, shaping the curve of her hip, tracing the flat plane of her stomach, the leisurely quest deliberately tantalising. His fingers seemed to linger everywhere, except where she most desired his caress. And he knew it.

From some whirling corner of her mind she realised that he could stretch out this waiting—this wanting—forever. He intended her to ask, to plead, this time.

Shall I make you beg me to take you? He'd asked her that once, some lifetime ago, and she had turned in scorn and panic from the very idea. Now she might be called on to pay for that rejection. And the price might cost her soul.

When at last—at long and screaming last—his fingers touched her lightly, almost questioningly, at the soft and pliant junction of her thighs, a moan of anticipation, almost of greed, burst from her taut throat.

She wanted suddenly to be free of the imprisoning denim which guarded her from him. She wanted to be free—to be naked in his arms.

Slowly he lifted her, steadied her so that she was no longer helpless in his embrace but standing facing him, a little way apart. Their eyes met in a strange, charged acknowledgement.

His asked. Hers answered. He moved, cancelling the space which separated them, as he took the loosened shirt and slipped it from her shoulders, letting it fall to the floor.

She tried to speak, but he shook his head, laying a silencing finger on her lips, before allowing his hand to trail without haste down her throat and between her tumescent breasts, to the clasp of her jeans.

And paused, his eyes going past her to stare at the door with sharp and frowning attention.

He said, half to himself, 'Someone's there . . .'

Just as he spoke, there was a brisk rapping at the heavy panels, and a voice called, 'Monsieur— Monsieur de Courcy! You are there? It is Madame Béthune. I have a message for you.'

The warm intensity of the past moments was shattered in a second.

Alain's brows lifted, and his mouth twisted cynically. He said, 'You must have a guardian angel, *ma femme*.' He picked up Philippa's shirt and tossed it to her. 'Now cover yourself while I see what she wants.'

Philippa fled to the stairs. On the small dark landing, she dressed herself with shaky haste, hearing although she could not see Madame Béthune's surge into the room.

'Monsieur de Courcy?' The good woman was clearly bewildered and a little indignant. 'But how is this? I understood you to be Monsieur de Thiéry. When we spoke on the telephone, that was the name I was given.'

There was a pause, then Alain said slowly, 'I am sorry if there has been a misunderstanding, *madame*. I am indeed Alain de Courcy, although it is true the original booking was made by—an associate of mine.'

'And Mademoiselle Roscoe—where is she?'

'I will call her.' Alain raised his voice. 'Philippa, come down, *chérie*. We have a visitor.'

Philippa descended the stairs reluctantly. She had been trembling so much, she wasn't sure whether she'd fastened all her buttons, or even united them with the correct buttonholes, and she was aware that her hair was tousled, and her breathing still flurried.

But she made herself smile as if she didn't have a care in the world, tensely aware of Alain's sardonic gaze. *'Bonsoir, madame.'*

'The little Philippa!' Madame's chins dropped in amazement. 'Oh, but you have changed so much, *petite!'* I would hardly have known you.' She flung her arms round her and embraced her warmly. 'And how is your dear father?'

'Very well. I hope he'll be joining me here soon.'

'Joining *us,* *chérie,'* Alain corrected silkily. 'Isn't it time you told Madame Béthune your news—that you and I are married?'

Madame's round dark eyes seemed to increase in diameter. 'You are married?' she exclaimed. 'Then this is a honeymoon, *enfin.'*

Alain sent an ironic look in his wife's rigid direction. 'Hardly that,' he said with a shrug. 'It is more—a working holiday.'

Madame Béthune emitted a squeak of amusement. 'Work, *monsieur*? But when a man and his young wife are alone together, they should think only of pleasure, isn't it so? You should not allow her to work. If I were in her shoes, it would be very different, I promise you.'

'You flatter me, *madame.'* Alain grinned at her, flirting good-humouredly. 'You wish to console me, perhaps?'

'With so new a bride, you should not need consolation.' Madame gave a gusty sigh. 'But if I were twenty years younger...' and she gave Alain a delicately ribald dig in the ribs with her elbow, and collapsed into a gale of mirth.

'But I forgot my errand,' she said at last, still shaking with laughter. 'I have had a telephone call from Monsieur Bartran at the garage. His brother has returned this evening from Bordeaux with the part for your car, *monsieur*. It will be fitted tomorrow.'

'*Merveilleux!*' Alain's smile flicked at Philippa. 'That's what we've been waiting to hear, isn't it, *chérie*?'

From some icy deep inside her, Philippa heard herself answer, 'Yes.'

'That is good.' Madame beamed at them both. 'And now I shall intrude no longer,' she added firmly, declining Alain's offers of coffee and wine. She embraced Philippa again. 'Be happy, my little one,' she commanded, and departed on a wave of goodwill.

Her departure was succeeded by a profound silence.

Alain broke it at last. 'You said a while ago that you were going to your room. Perhaps you should do so.' There was no emotion at all in his voice, or, when she dared look at him, his face.

'Is that—what you want?' She couldn't believe she had actually said that. Had she really so little pride, so little self-respect?

He shrugged again. 'What I want,' he said with cool and deadly emphasis, 'is to drive away from here tomorrow as soon as my car is fixed.' The green eyes grazed her mockingly. 'After all, *ma belle*, it was—only a kiss.'

She whispered, 'Yes—of course.' Then she turned and went away from him, back upstairs into the darkness.

CHAPTER ELEVEN

THE darkness was everywhere. It swirled around her, suffocating her. And it was within her, consuming her in pain and loneliness.

Only a kiss. The words seemed to be etched on her mind in letters of fire. That was how little it had meant to Alain. She had been on the verge of giving herself completely, and without reservation, for the first time—but even so, he would still have driven away tomorrow without a backward glance.

And it was no use reminding herself that Alain's departure was what she'd wanted—what she'd urged on him. By coming here, she had intended to separate herself from Alain once and for all. Now he was prepared to gratify her wish.

It had to be, she told herself vehemently, over and over again. She couldn't accept a continuation of their marriage on the terms he was offering. She wasn't prepared to occupy the fringe of his attention, waiting to be noticed when he could spare the time like— Patient Griselda or some other wimp.

And when they parted, she would have nothing to reproach herself for. Nothing to remember with shame. That had to be her comfort.

There was no sign of him when she eventually ventured downstairs in the morning. For a moment she thought, stunned, that he had already gone without even a goodbye, but a swift check in his room revealed that his clothes and toilet articles were still there, half packed. He must be down in Montascaux standing impatiently over the mechanics.

She took her coffee to the studio, and made her preparations for the day. She looked long and critically at Alain's portrait. Maybe it was wishful thinking, but it seemed to her to be the best thing she had ever done. But perhaps that was because she was seeing it with the eyes of love, she thought wistfully.

An hour later, she heard the sound of the car. Her heart jolted and she began to alter a highlight with savage concentration. Eventually he came up the stairs and stood in the doorway.

She said, too brightly, 'Is the car fixed?'

'It's fine.'

'Then I suppose you'll be off now.' She made a business of altering the position of the easel.

'Soon,' he said. 'I thought you wanted me to give another sitting.'

Philippa shrugged. 'I don't want to cause you any inconvenience.'

'You won't.' He walked to her side and looked at the canvas. 'Is there much else to do?'

'Not with this one,' she said. 'I can finish the rest from memory, if necessary.' God how achingly true that was!

'I see.' Alain's face was quizzical. 'I did you an injustice, *ma femme*, when I tried to dissuade you from continuing your studies. You have real talent. I hope that you develop it to its full.' His smile was friendly, but it contained an element of dismissal—set her at a distance, and she knew it. 'Will you sell me this painting?'

She shook her head. 'Not this one. With this, I came of age as a painter. I'm sure you understand.'

'I don't think that understanding has ever played a great part in our relationship,' he said gravely. 'But I promise to try.' He paused. 'So—what about this final sitting? Do you want me to strip for you?'

Philippa swallowed. It sounded deafeningly loud in the sudden quiet of the studio. She tried to smile. 'You—you don't mean it, surely?'

'Why not? It would be a new experience for me— as for most men—to take my clothes off for a woman who has no interest in me except as a composition of light and shade, of planes and angles.' He gave her a mocking look. 'Isn't that how it is, *ma chère*?'

'Well—yes.' Her heart was hammering.

'So why don't you ask me, then?' He paused. 'Or is my body not interesting enough for you? You feel, maybe, that you know me too well?'

She lifted the canvas carefully off the easel, not looking at him. 'It—isn't that.'

Dear God, she thought, almost hysterically, she didn't know him at all. Not in that way.

She managed a ghost of a laugh. 'You've—rather taken me by surprise. But if this is a serious offer, Alain, then of course I'd like to make some drawings of you. I—I do need the practice,' she added lamely.

'We seem to be surprising each other,' he said. He glanced round. 'I presume you wish to alter the setting?'

They moved the table away, and arranged a make-shift platform with boxes and some old gold brocade curtains Philippa had discovered in a packing case the previous day. She spent some time over the brocade, pulling at its folds, making it fall just as she wanted, aware of a feeling of total unreality.

Oh, God, she thought, I shouldn't be doing this—I shouldn't be allowing it to happen. Because I can't be objective. I can't just treat it as a useful exercise.

She turned away and picked up her sketching block, her hands trembling. She'd never, she thought, actually looked at Alain naked before. Not really. That first time, she had been too embarrassed and angry—and since then their few encounters had been in the dark. This would be a moment of truth for her.

And it had arrived, she realised, as he said, 'I'm ready.'

Philippa turned slowly to face him. He was—magnificent. There was no other word for it. Hands on hips, head slightly thrown back, he endured her fascinated, almost obsessive scrutiny.

'Are you going to draw me, *ma belle*, or commit me to memory?'

She started, faint colour flaring in her face. 'Oh, will you sit, please—and turn sideways a little? Drop your shoulder. No, that's too much.'

'It would be simpler if you showed me.'

She hesitated momentarily, then went over to him, putting her hands on his warm shoulders and manipulating him into the position she wanted, savouring as she did so the silken smoothness of his skin, and the firm play of muscle in his back and arms.

She said, 'Now this time you must tell me if you get tired—or cold.'

'Or even too warm, perhaps.' His tone was laconic. 'Do you know something, *chérie*? I think this is the first time you've ever touched me of your own accord.'

Philippa snatched her hands away. 'Remember the pose, please,' she said, and went back to her drawing board.

She made a number of false starts, crumpling sheet after sheet and throwing them away.

'Is something wrong?' Alain asked at last. 'You seem disturbed. Shall I get dressed and find you a nice safe vase of flowers instead?'

She gritted her teeth. 'No, thanks. Maybe the pose is wrong—too forced.'

Alain sat up, shrugging. 'Then that is easily remedied.' He turned on his side, propping himself on his elbow, one long leg bent, and slightly drawn up. He smiled at her. 'Is that better?'

'Yes,' she admitted unwillingly. He looked totally relaxed, as much at ease as if he'd been posing nude all his life.

I wish I could be equally casual, she thought.

She tried to assume a clinical detachment as she studied him, observing how the lean, elegant lines of his body had gained a new grace, bone and muscle flowing in total harmony.

At the same time, she realised, there was something watchful about the position he had taken up—something anticipatory, even predatory. It was reflected in the smile which still played about his mouth, and in his hooded eyes. It was intriguing—almost mysterious.

Shaken by sudden excitement, she thought, My God, if I can only capture this!

This time she didn't fumble or fudge the lines. Her pencil seemed to sing across the paper, her hand and eye working in perfect co-ordination. She had to do this, she thought feverishly. She couldn't lose it. Not now.

'May I rest a little?' Her consent taken for granted, Alain sat up and reached for his trousers.

Unwillingly Philippa put down her pencil, aware of the tension in her own shoulder and neck muscles, of the trickle of perspiration between her breasts.

'Am I permitted to look?' Alain came to stand behind her.

'When it's finished,' she said huskily. His hands were resting lightly on her shoulders, but the touch seemed to scorch her to the bone. It was too reminiscent of the previous night, she thought restively.

'It is time you took a break too.' His fingers moved, testing, exploring. 'You're tied up in knots.'

Gently at first, then more forcefully, he began to massage the aching muscles at the base of her neck.

She tried to pull away. 'I'm all right, really.'

'Tais-toi,' he said. 'Let me do this for you.'

With a sigh of capitulation, Philippa gave herself up to his ministrations. His touch was magic, she thought wonderingly, intimate yet impersonal at the same time in some strange way.

But, healing though his hands undoubtedly were, the stroking, kneading movements were creating other strains, other tensions elsewhere in her body.

'Relax,' he ordered softly.

But how could she, when, once more, her entire being was responding—coming alive under his touch.

She felt his fingers move over her shoulder, and feather along her collarbones, before sliding down to release the buttons on her shirt.

'No!' She put up a hand to stop him.

'Sois tranquille,' he said. 'Trust me.'

The shirt slipped off her shoulders, and down to her waist. His fingers were on her naked spine, and the muscles which flanked it, stroking and smoothing.

Her bared skin flushed and tingled under the play of his hands. Her body began to arch in pleasure, her small breasts swelling with sharp sensitivity. Tiny sparks danced behind her closed eyelids.

Trust him, he'd said, but the betrayal was coming once more from herself. From the savage urgency of her unfulfilled body.

Then, with stark suddenness, it was over. The warm fingers stopped stroking her body, and moved almost briskly to pull her shirt back into place.

'Voilà.' His tone was almost casual. He picked up her drawing block and pencil and handed them to her. 'Shall we continue?'

He walked back to the makeshift dais, pausing only to shed his trousers, and lay down again, effortlessly assuming his former position.

Philippa stared at the drawing in front of her until the lines blurred. She was shaking so much that she could hardly hold the pencil, and her mouth felt dry. She was running a fever—burning up. The ache deep inside her had expanded into pain—into a hunger she could no longer deny—a hunger which demanded assuagement, no matter what it might cost.

She let the drawing board fall and stood up, tugging at the buttons on her shirt until they gave way. One of them tore. Unheeding, she shrugged off the garment and let it drop to the ground.

Alain did not speak or move, but in the hectic silence, she heard the rasp of a suddenly indrawn breath as he watched her.

She kicked off her sandals and trod barefoot across the space that divided them.

The green eyes were watchful, guarded as he looked up at her. He said softly, *'Et alors, madame?'*

Her hands fumbled with the fastening of her jeans. The material clung, encumbering her, and she thought she would never be rid of it. But at last it was done. Her remaining covering was little more than a brief lacy triangle, but she stripped that away too.

Then she dropped to her knees beside him, her hand reaching to touch, shyly, tentatively, the muscular sweep of his bare thigh. 'Alain?' Her voice trembled into life. 'Alain, *je t'en prie—je t'implore*!'

Shall I make you beg me to take you? His mocking question was now being answered at last by her total surrender.

He said harshly, 'Ah, *Dieu*!' and his hands took her fiercely, drawing her down beside him on to the folds of gold brocade.

His mouth was a flame, consuming her, and she yielded deliriously to its demands, her body pressed against the length of his, savouring the intimate delight of the contact.

He lifted himself away from her slightly, his hands stroking down her body, lingering on each curve and contour as if he was learning her through his finger-tips. Then the dark head bent so that his lips could caress her breasts. The flick of his tongue across the roused, rosy peaks sent needle-points of white-hot sensation shafting through her inmost being.

She moaned with pleasure, running her own hands in turn down his back, across the taut, flat buttocks to his narrow flanks.

His response was urgent and immediate, his mouth returning to hers, his hand sliding down to part her thighs, and seek the secret places of her womanhood, so long denied to him.

He touched her delicately at first, his fingers a mere whisper of sensation against her satin heat, then deepened the caress with a warm and deliberate sensuality, beckoning her down a path she had never traversed before.

Her eyes were wide and cloudy with excitement as she lay, looking up at him, every quivering nerve-ending attuned to this new and dangerous enchantment.

He smiled at her, then his head bent, and his mouth possessed her instead with slow, devastating insistence.

The breath caught raggedly in her throat. He couldn't be doing this to her. He couldn't . . .

Her senses were fainting, her body drowning in a warm rippling pleasure which was carrying her inexorably to some edge—some terrifying brink.

Her head fell back, and her body arched helplessly, rent apart by shafts of delight so intense she thought she would die. There were tears on her face. She was aware of Alain moving, and his body covering hers. Acting on pure instinct, her arms went up to lock round his neck, while her slender legs lifted to hold and weld him close to her.

Such a long time. The words sobbed inside her. Such an eternity since this.

She felt him inside her, steel masked in velvet, and cried out in joy and welcome, her embrace tightening convulsively as he began to move, thrusting deeper and deeper inside her.

She was content for it to be like this—to give herself at last. But then suddenly, amazingly, she experienced the swift dark surge of her own returning pleasure. The world of reason slid away, and in the warm,

swirling ecstatic void which replaced it there was—
only and forever—Alain.

Philippa opened drowsily reluctant eyelids to find
herself lying in a welter of gold.

For a moment she was completely disorientated,
telling herself confusedly that she must be still asleep
and dreaming, then reality began to impinge, and she
saw her golden world for what it was. She began to
remember...

Untrammelled late afternoon sun was pouring in
through the windows of the *pigeonnier*, illuminating
every corner and crevice with warm syrupy light.

And Philippa herself was lying on the floor, completely swathed in the folds of the gold brocade.

She sat up slowly, pushing her hair out of her eyes,
assimilating other details. Her own clothes, folded,
had been acting as her pillow, but she had not the
vaguest recollection of putting them there.

And, more significantly, she was alone.

Her sense of delicious lassitude began to evaporate.
Where, she wondered, was Alain?

She'd wanted him to be there when she woke, she
realised. Wanted the reassurance of his arms round
her, and his lips on hers.

And more than anything, she thought, a warm wave
of colour sweeping over her, she had wanted him to
make love to her again, to ravish her body with his,
exquisitely and completely, to make her cry out in
abandonment as he took her, once more, to the heights
of culmination.

I've probably exhausted him, she thought with
mingled guilt and delight.

She had lost count of the times they'd made love. One lingering, sensuous act had seemed to flow naturally into the next, as they discovered new ways to pleasure each other.

She'd never imagined, even in her wildest dreams, that she would be capable of such depths of feeling. But, at the same time, she acknowledged wonderingly that it was only Alain who could have liberated her emotions with such totality.

She stretched, frankly enjoying the various unfamiliar aches and pains that her body was making her aware of. Her muscles weren't used to such prolonged exercise, she thought with a little grin. And the studio floor had been hard, although both of them had been too far gone in rapture to care.

If Alain had gone to find somewhere more comfortable to sleep, then she couldn't altogether blame him.

Her drawing-board was lying where she had dropped it, and she picked it up, studying her drawing with smiling eyes.

I won't finish it, she thought. I'll have it framed, just as it is, and keep it somewhere totally private to remind me of today—the beginning of the rest of my life with Alain.

She tucked the board under her arm and went, with one last lingering glance at the sunlit room, down the stairs.

She had half expected to find Alain in the living-room. She'd grown used to the almost perpetual aroma of coffee when he was around. But the room was empty. There was no sound in the house. In fact, no sign of life at all, so he must be very deeply asleep. Wherever he was.

Philippa put the drawing down on the table and went upstairs.

She pushed open Alain's door, and stood for an endless moment as her shocked mind tried to assimilate what she saw.

The room was deserted—bare. All Alain's things were gone, and the bed was stripped once more down to the mattress, the duvet and bedding folded neatly at its foot.

Her hand caught at the doorpost, the knuckles turning white. She heard her voice, strained, almost unrecognisable, saying, 'No—oh God, please—no!'

But denial, however fervent, was useless. Without the slightest doubt, Alain had gone—just as he'd promised he would. And nothing that had happened between them—the breathless, seeking urgency that knew no satiation, the frantic overwhelming pleasure—had made the slightest difference to his resolve.

She flew downstairs, jerking open the front door, but there was no car in the courtyard beyond. Slowly she sank down until she was half kneeling, half crouching in the doorway. The warmth of the sun on her face seemed to be mocking her now.

She wanted to cry, but no tears would come.

How could he have gone like that, without a word? Yes, they had agreed to part, to separate permanently, but that was a lifetime ago. Didn't he know how she'd changed? How she now felt?

The unacceptable truth facing her was—of course he knew, but it made no difference. Alain was probably all too accustomed to evoking that level of response from his women. With him, love was not an issue, as he'd made cynically clear. He'd had her, and enjoyed her, and that was it.

He'd have enjoyed the victory too, she thought desolately. He'd have relished breaking down her defences, destroying her stubborn resistance, and reducing her to the level of a small, sobbing wanton animal.

I like to win. Only last night he had told her that. She got stiffly to her feet and walked over to the table. That was what she'd seen in her drawing, heaven help her, but in her excitement she had failed to realise its significance.

How pathetically easy she'd been to manipulate!

She unclipped the drawing from the board and tore it again and again until it was utterly destroyed. Then she gathered up the fragments, took them to the stove and watched them burn.

She was burning too—with humiliation, and regret. Dear God, hadn't she had enough warnings?

And now she would have to leave too. She couldn't stay here in the house in the clouds. Not with these memories. She would have to move on, find somewhere else to rent, put her life back together somehow before Gavin returned.

She would pack her things, walk down to Montascaux and take the first bus to anywhere.

She'd tackle the studio first, she thought. Meet the pain head-on.

She wouldn't be able to carry all her equipment. Some of it would have to stay here. Maybe she'd be able to come back for it, later. When she could stand it.

It took a long time to bring her painting things down from the *pigeonnier*. Even though the easel folded up, it was still heavy and difficult to manoeuvre on the narrow stairs, and she was glad of this, because it made her concentrate on the job in hand, and left no room for other thinking.

She left her unused canvases. The portrait of Alain at the table she turned to the wall.

She was about to go upstairs to her room and fling her clothes into her bag when she heard the sound of the car. She paused, tensing, staring out through the open door.

Alain's car, she thought, her throat muscles tightening agonisingly. But it couldn't be. It was an hallucination. Alain had gone, and he wasn't coming back.

As if paralysed, she watched him climb out from the driving seat and cross the courtyard towards the door.

She didn't know why he'd come back, and she didn't want to know. The only certainty was that she couldn't face him—couldn't see the triumph in his eyes—or the pity.

She tried to slam the door, her hands fumbling for the massive key in the lock, but as she did so, Alain reached it and pushed it open, using his shoulder.

'Are you crazy?' he demanded roughly, as she backed away from him. He looked around, his brows lifting. 'Why is your painting gear down here?'

'Because I'm leaving.' Her voice cracked a little. 'Travelling on. I'll make sure you have an address eventually—for the lawyers.'

'For the lawyers,' he repeated slowly. 'What in the name of God are you talking about?'

'The divorce.' Philippa lifted her chin. 'That's what we agreed, wasn't it? So there's nothing more to be said. I—I can't imagine why you chose to come back.'

For a moment he was silent. He was very white, she saw, and there was a tiny muscle jerking beside his mouth. Then he smiled.

'*D'accord*. As you say, *madame*. There is nothing more. I'd thought, maybe, we should say *adieu*—but I will not detain you any longer.'

Head held high, Philippa went past him, and up the stairs to her room. She opened the door, and stood, aghast. It was in such turmoil that, for a moment, she thought the unthinkable had happened in this backwater—that a thief had got in.

Then, slowly, it dawned on her what the mess confronting her consisted of.

It was Alain's clothes, she realised, stunned, her eyes roving over the sweaters, shirts and casual trousers, strewn across her bed. And over on the dressing chest, his brushes and razor. The leather toilet bag he used for travelling.

She heard him follow her upstairs and turned slowly.

His face expressionless, he said with cold formality, '*Je vous demand pardon*. I was—presumptuous. Perhaps it would be simpler if I packed first.'

He made to move past her, and Philippa caught his arm.

She said hoarsely, 'Why did you put your things in my room?'

'Do you really need to ask?' There was a wrenched harshness in his voice that caught at her heart. 'Because I thought—I hoped that, at last, I would be sleeping here tonight. That from now on you would be spending every night in my arms.' He gave a bitter laugh. 'What a fool I was! Because it meant nothing to you, did it, *ma femme*, that—heaven that we shared together only an hour or two ago.' He shook her hand from his arm. 'Be good enough not to touch me.'

'Alain, no, listen to me.' Her hands gripped the front of his shirt, clung. 'I thought you'd gone—that you'd left me. You said you would, as soon as the car was fixed. I woke up alone, and your room was empty, and the car had gone. I—I didn't look in here. I didn't think . . .' She took a deep breath. 'I was so unhappy, I wanted to die. That's why I was leaving. Because I couldn't bear to stay here without you.'

The green eyes narrowed in disbelief, but he didn't push her away. 'Leave you? You truly thought that?' He shook his head. 'No, *mon amour*. Whatever I may have said, I never had the least intention of going. Even without the intervention of Monsieur de Thiéry, I would have found some excuse to stay, until I got what I came for.'

'What was that?' Her voice was barely more than a whisper.

A smile twisted his lips. 'It was you, my reluctant wife. All of you, body, heart and sweet, stubborn mind.' His hands covered hers, and she realised they were trembling. He said, 'Philippa, don't pretend any more. You know that I love you. Will you stay here with me—share the honeymoon we never had? Begin our marriage all over again?'

She said brokenly, 'Alain, it's you that's pretending. It's not me that you want. It's the Baronne—Marie-Laure—and I—I can't live with that, no matter how much I love you. It's too much to ask.'

He said gently, 'But I don't ask it, *mon amour*. Marie-Laure means nothing to me, and never did. Oh, yes, when I first met her she was alluring—an exciting adventure, but that was all.'

'How can you say that?' she whispered. 'Alain, I saw you together—at that party, on the terrace. You know that. You—you were kissing her and . . .'

'Ah, no.' He gathered her into his arms, held her against him, his lips against her hair. 'It was over—all over between us long before. She followed me—threw herself at me. Treated me like the fool I must have seemed. Only by that time, of course, I knew . . .'

'Knew what?' Philippa's voice was a thread.

'That like your friend Fabrice, she had been hired, in the first instance, by my uncle,' he said grimly. He met the incredulity in her eyes, and nodded. 'You find it hard to credit? So did I—at first. I have my share of male vanity, you understand? I met this beautiful woman who made it clear she wanted me, and I believed, to begin with, everything she wished me to believe.'

He smiled cynically. 'When the scandal broke, I was astonished. I was not, after all, the first man in her life. It was all—too neat, somehow. So I had enquiries made, and discovered that she was heavily in debt. The Baron was a wealthy man, but not a generous one. And Marie-Laure liked to gamble. There wasn't a casino in the South of France that she hadn't visited. For my uncle, she was the perfect weapon. So I ended the *affaire*.'

He paused. 'I had, of course, the perfect excuse. I was going to be married.'

Philippa said bleakly. 'I see.'

'No.' A laugh shook in his voice. 'You do not see, *ma femme*, and you never have.' He cupped her face in his hands. 'Since that evening in Lowden Square when I first saw you, there has been no one in my life. No one but you. Don't you know that?'

'No. How can I know it? I was an expedient for you. I wasn't beautiful. I didn't belong in your world...'

'Not beautiful?' he questioned softly. 'Ah, Philippa, for an artist, you can be very blind. And what does the world I belong to know of the kind of love and loyalty you had to offer? I found myself thinking—tonight, she only thinks of her father. One day, perhaps, she will think of me.'

She felt his heart thudding against her. He said unevenly, 'I could not believe what was happening to me. The next morning, at the hotel, I was in agony, asking myself what I would do if you did not agree, if you did not come to me. Knowing that, wherever you went, I would follow. As I did when you left me.'

She looked into his eyes, saw her own pain, her own uncertainty mirrored there. She said, with a little gasp, 'Alain...'

His arms went round her fiercely, holding her so that their bodies ground together. His mouth on hers was heatedly passionate—demanding, questioning, and Philippa answered with her heart on her lips.

When he lifted his head, his eyes were emerald-bright, the flame in them scorching her. 'Tell me you love me,' he said. 'Say it. Say you will be my wife in truth, this time, and that you'll never leave me again.'

'But it was you who kept leaving,' she protested, her fingers shyly stroking his face. 'In Paris, I was always alone. There were all those nights you didn't stay at the apartment...'

'Do you think I could bear to be there with you?' Alain demanded roughly. 'Watching you hating me—

shrinking every time I came near you. I didn't blame
you for that. I'd intended to wait, to be patient, and
instead, I behaved like an idiot and a brute.'

He groaned. 'All that time in London, I had hardly
dared allow myself to touch your hand in case I
frightened you away. On our wedding night, the
knowledge that you belonged to me at last made me
forget everything else. I was crazy with wanting you,
and so sure that I could make you want me in return.

'Afterwards, I hated myself. I didn't sleep for the
rest of the night. All I could see were your wounded
eyes, *ma chère*. All I could think was that I'd ruined
everything between us forever.

'There's a suite of rooms at the company building
for use in emergency. I started sleeping there at night.
I had to stay away, because I couldn't trust myself to
be near you. You only seemed prepared to tolerate
the minimum contact between us, and there were times
I needed much more than that, and I was scared I
might shock you—disgust you—create even worse
barriers between us.'

'And I thought you were with Marie-Laure.'
Philippa looked up at him reproachfully. 'And you
let me think so, Alain. You gave the impression you
were still having an affair.'

He grimaced ruefully. 'Well, perhaps—a little. Your
hostility about her intrigued me. It made me wonder
if you could actually be jealous—if, under all that
polite neutrality you showed me most of the time, you
were beginning to care. It was the only hope I had to
cling to. I kept telling myself that if you were really
as indifferent to me as you made out, then my having
an *affaire* shouldn't affect you as it obviously did. So
I decided to lead you on a little. And Marie-Laure

helped, of course, in her determined attempts to get me back again.'

He bent his head and kissed her very gently. 'Can you forgive me? If I hurt you, I was more than repaid when I thought you'd fallen in love with Fabrice. Then I began to know what jealousy really is, and I suffered. I also realised that by dangling Marie-Laure in front of you as bait, I'd trapped only myself. You were distressingly eager to free me so that I could marry her, and then, when I tried to explain—to tell you the truth—you wouldn't listen.'

'I thought that was what you wanted. A real marriage with the woman you loved.'

'It was you that I meant. It was our marriage I wanted to be real, but I would have had you under any terms—any conditions. I'd have spent the rest of our life together wooing you, praying that one day you'd turn to me.' He sighed. 'I thought maybe if we had children, and you cared for them, you might eventually come to love their father. That's how desperate I was.'

'I was desperate too,' she confessed in a low voice. 'That's why I ran away. I—I couldn't take any more. And today, when I thought you'd left me, I wanted to die.'

'You were sleeping so sweetly I thought I'd have time to complete my errands and return before you knew I'd been away,' Alain said wryly. 'I had phone calls to make to Paris—to tell colleagues I was taking an extended leave, and that as it was my honeymoon I did not wish to be disturbed. Also we needed more food. I have to keep up my strength, you understand.'

'Do you?' She gave him a limpid look.

'Why, yes, *mignonne*. It's very tough work being an artist's model. Particularly when one is obliged to make love to the artist.'

'Oh God!' Philippa clapped a hand to her mouth. 'I've just remembered—I tore it up—that beautiful drawing of you.'

'Well, I'll make sure you have plenty of opportunity to draw me again, if you wish.' He kissed the tip of her nose. 'I do not intend to wear many clothes over the next week or two.'

'Is that all the time we have?' she asked wistfully.

'No,' he said. 'After we leave here, we are flying to the States to bring your father home. He can come with us to Fontainebleu, and rest up there for a while.'

'I hope finding out that I'm married won't be too much of a shock for him,' Philippa said worriedly.

'Maybe when he sees how happy we are, he'll forgive us both.'

'And are we going to be happy?' she asked demurely.

'Very.' Alain kissed her mouth softly. 'We have nothing to do, after all, but eat, drink, enjoy the sunlight—and each other.'

'And I shall paint, of course,' she reminded him, then grimaced. 'I shall have to move all my gear back to the studio again.'

'Later,' he said. He took her hands and carried them to the buttons of his shirt. 'After our wedding night.'

She said breathlessly, unfastening the buttons with fingers that shook a little, 'But our wedding night was ages ago.'

'Au contraire, mon amour.' His hands stroked down her body, creating the first warm ripples of pleasure. 'It begins now, and with your permission, it is going

to last a very long time.' His lips hovered a tantalising hair's breadth from hers. 'Do you agree?'

'Yes, my darling.' Philippa looked up into her husband's eyes with love and perfect trust. 'Oh, yes, Alain—*Alain* . . .'

And, after that, there was no more need for words.

HARLEQUIN ◆ PRESENTS®

A Year Down Under

Beginning in January 1993, some of Harlequin Presents's most exciting authors will join us as we celebrate the land down under by featuring one title per month set in Australia or New Zealand.

Intense, passionate romances, these stories will take you from the heart of the Australian outback to the wilds of New Zealand, from the sprawling cattle and sheep stations to the sophistication of cities like Sydney and Auckland.

Share the adventure—and the romance— of A Year Down Under!

Don't miss our first visit in HEART OF THE OUTBACK by Emma Darcy, Harlequin Presents #1519, available in January wherever Harlequin Books are sold.   YDU-G